What the Zhang Boys Know

WHAT THE ZHANG BOYS KNOW

A Novel in Stories

CLIFFORD GARSTANG

Press 53
Winston-Salem

Press 53, LLC
PO Box 30314
Winston-Salem, NC 27130

First Edition

Cover art, "Night in Blue" Copyright © 2012
by Benjamin Williamson, used by permission of the artist.
www.BenWill.com

Author photo by Carol Turrentine

Library of Congress Control Number: 2012909930

Printed on acid-free paper
ISBN 978-1-935708-61-2

Only on the firm foundation of unyielding despair,
can the soul's habitation henceforth be safely built.

~ Bertrand Russell

ACKNOWLEDGMENTS

"Nanking Mansion" appeared in *GSU Review*, Spring/Summer 2007
"Counterpoint" appeared in *Wisconsin Review*, Vol. 43, No. 2, Spring 2009
"Hunger" appeared in *Cream City Review*, Vol. 33, No. 1, Spring 2009
"Artoyen's Razor" appeared in *Tampa Review*, No. 40, Fall 2010
"Last Lilacs" appeared in *FRiGG*, No. 30, Fall 2010
"The Replacement Wife" appeared in *Blackbird*, Vol. 10, No. 2, Fall 2011
"The Face in the Window" appeared in *Valparaiso Fiction Review*, Vol. 1, No. 1, Winter 2011
"The Shrine to His Ancestors" appeared in *Prime Mincer*, Vol. 1, No. 3, Winter 2011
"A Hole in the Wall" appeared in *Bellevue Literary Review*, Vol. 12, No. 1, Spring 2012

WHAT THE ZHANG BOYS KNOW

NANKING MANSION

1

How did it happen that every person Zhang Feng-qi knows in America is in the same place at the same time?

Clustered at one end of the wide, high-ceilinged hallway—known to the building's residents as the "Gallery" for its large, abstract canvases—there they all stand: Feng-qi's father, newly arrived from China, who only a month ago struggled to fill the meaningless days of his Shanghai widowerhood; Feng-qi's two sons, with their hybrid features, hazel eyes, pale yellow skin, and hair that is almost, but not quite, black; his dour, gray-suited mother-in-law, or, more precisely, the mother of his late wife, Maddie, who, Feng-qi suspects, also hovers nearby, amused by the chaos she knows makes his knees tremble. And in the background: his pasty, mustachioed neighbors, the two men who live together in the next apartment and might be homosexuals, but, since Feng-qi does not know how such men behave and thus has no basis for comparison, he can't be certain; another neighbor, from the far end of the Gallery, a reclusive painter, the creator of one of the hallway abstracts, with spatters of paint on his jeans and bare feet; the skeletal, wild-haired sculptor from apartment Number 3 who always works (or so it seems to Feng-qi, who has observed the man work on a few occasions, and invariably it was the same) with a smoldering cigarette clutched between his yellowed teeth, ash raining on his unfathomable creations of twisted timber and clay; the young, blank-eyed couple, constantly hand-holding, or arm-locked, entwined, as if each draws energy from the other's touch; and the fat Armenian, the developer who resurrected this building, the Nanking Mansion, a 1920's tenement on the racially tense edge of D.C.'s Chinatown, converted into over-priced artists' lofts in which Feng-qi and his family had somehow (Feng-qi no longer remembers how or why except that it was his wife's idea for them to mingle with artsy people, as if their own lives of mathematics and public policy were too uncreative an environment in which to raise their sons) come to live amidst a flock of flamboyant painters and sculptors and writers. Even Feng-qi's boss is there, a Labor Department bureaucrat who has stopped by with work for Feng-qi, an accordion file with "Frank" boldly scrawled on the side (Feng-qi's co-workers in the Bureau of Statistics call him "Frank," uniformly unable or unwilling to bend their throats around the unfamiliar vowel and consonant combinations and vaguely uncertain, even after all the time he's toiled among them, whether "Zhang" or "Feng-qi" is his given name, knowing, or thinking they know, that Chinese names are the inverse of American names), containing a statistical comparison of unemployment in four urban markets, which the Secretary needs immediately, before Monday if possible, even though Feng-qi has taken these few days of his annual leave to help his father get better settled after an initially rocky start to his life in America.

No, not quite everyone he knows. Jessica Lee—the Chinese woman from Olsson's Books on 5th Street who, even before Maddie's accident, had caught his eye, not in any illicit or unsavory way, but by virtue of her being Chinese, that's all it had been at first—Jessica Lee isn't there. She *is*, though, due any minute. Feng-qi looks at his watch.

2

When Feng-qi's wife died there weren't many options for the household. He could juggle his job with the cooking and cleaning, barely. The three-level condo—his wife's choice, the last unit she inspected after viewing dozens of candidates when they decided the time had arrived to become homeowners—was expansive, but spare and easy to maintain, with minimal furniture since it was so much larger than the two-bedroom flat they'd been renting in Cleveland Park. But someone had to take care of his sons. Simon had just started kindergarten, Wesley wasn't yet old enough for the D.C. Chinatown Community Center's pre-school, and both—especially since the accident, and the jolt of being told by a neighbor, while Feng-qi was still at the hospital dealing with his own sudden grief, that their mother would not be coming home—needed considerable supervision and attention. Feng-qi had tried everything: a babysitter, employed from the stratified bulletin board in the cafeteria at work, who demanded cab fare from Georgetown and back on top of her lofty hourly fee because she felt unsafe in the Zhangs' not-quite-gentrified neighborhood and who, more problematically, resembled, to the boys' horror, a child-eating fairytale witch; old Mrs. Wong from the retirement home at 4th and H, who had trouble remembering the boys' names and chain-smoked Camel cigarettes, one afternoon falling asleep on the couch and waking, miraculously, in time to extinguish a smoldering cushion; an acquaintance's teenage daughter, hired despite multiple tattoos and facial piercings, until she arrived at the condo one morning noticeably stoned. He even asked the beanpole sculptor to watch the boys—although Simon was afraid of the man because, the boy said, he looked like a snake standing up on his tail—until Feng-qi walked into the artist's studio one day to find tiny, three-year-old Wesley attacking a mound of clay with a knife in one hand and what looked to Feng-qi like a screwdriver in the other.

In desperation, Feng-qi called his mother-in-law.

3

As a graduate student at Berkeley (where in the bowels of the library, in a dim corner in which they both regularly sought attention-focusing quiet, he'd first summoned the courage to speak to Maddie, a statuesque blond political science major with plans to work on Capitol Hill after graduation or, failing that, land a career-deferring place in law school) it never occurred to him that he would one day marry an American girl. His parents didn't necessarily want him to come home to Shanghai to wed. After all, it was their dream that had pushed him to learn English and apply for the scholarship that brought him to the States. But they did expect him to meet a nice Chinese girl in California, to get a green card, to find his footing in America, while remaining at all times Chinese. That way he would have the best of both worlds, and if China returned to chaos, if the Red Guard rose again, at least *their* family would still have a future. If not, then, with its palpable, throbbing energy and endless social and economic opportunities for a handsome, American-educated Chinese boy, Shanghai beckoned.

After the Tiananmen Square massacre, though, everything changed. Feng-qi couldn't go home, even if he wanted to. He'd signed petitions. He'd marched in Berkeley campus protests against the brutal repression in his country. He'd even made speeches denouncing the regime, climbing atop a makeshift platform of milk crates, shouting his democracy demands in Chinese and then self-translating, with as much embellishment as his English could accommodate, for the mostly American, mostly accidental and ambivalent audience. He no longer felt as connected to China, despite his beloved parents and his native tongue, and the next time he met Maddie in the library stacks he looked at her with new appreciation. They progressed from talking about school and the balmy weather to more intimate exchanges: his fear of assassination by the Chinese secret police because of his unwise but sincere political activities; her parents' divorce when she was in high school, that had sent her into a year-long depression and one half-hearted wrist slashing; Feng-qi's belief that his mother, under pressure of China's one-child policy and his family's tenuous finances, had abandoned a second, unauthorized baby; Maddie's recent loss of her father to a fast-moving cancer that had devoured his kidneys and spread into his brain.

When Feng-qi wrote home about their engagement, in a rambling letter that was more difficult to compose than his thesis had been, it was weeks before he received a reply. Terse and marginally congratulatory, the note from his mother carried with it, as surely as if photographs had been enclosed in the envelope, images of what he knew had preceded its writing: his parents' cold, two-room flat, filled with boisterous grief; pots banging in the kitchen, like bells of mourning; bitter tea sloshed disbelievingly into chipped cups; and, finally, grudging, muttered acquiescence.

He and Maddie had told her mother about the engagement together, face-to-face, over brunch during one of Mrs. Martin's frequent visits from the East Coast, usually involving a swing through the wine country, and were met not just with silence—he could have understood silence, or shrieking, or arguments—but with denial. She ignored them. She resumed talking about the garden show she'd just attended, the aphids on her roses, the azaleas she wanted to plant, her neighbors' gaudy hydrangeas, about the spicy Pinot Noir she'd discovered in Sonoma, as if she hadn't just heard that her only daughter, her high-cheekboned, naturally blond, Phi Beta Kappa, headed-for-great-things daughter was marrying a Chinese immigrant. It was unthinkable, out of the question, impossible—and therefore she couldn't possibly have heard it; they couldn't have said it.

Even after they moved East and the boys were born, Simon within a year of the wedding and Wesley two years later, Maddie's mother never accepted Feng-qi. Maddie and Feng-qi loved living in D.C. and took advantage of all it had to offer, the museums, the parks. On Sundays, after services at the Episcopal church Maddie had joined and Feng-qi visited out of curiosity, they enjoyed strapping the boys into strollers and circling the flag-waving monuments on the Mall along with the tourists. They frequently invited Maddie's mother to visit and join them on these outings. She never did. And when Maddie lost control of her Honda on the Beltway—she'd been headed out to Rockville to visit her prep-school friend Kate, and Feng-qi thanked the gods every day that the boys had at the last minute refused to go with their mother—Mrs. Martin blamed him that her only child, the light of her life, was gone and she was alone in the world. Never mind that his soul had been wrenched from him, that he felt the wind pass through his body as if he had been split open, that his innocent boys were motherless. She blamed him for everything. Not that she said so, because they never actually had a conversation, about that or anything else, but there'd been her chilling glower when she came down from New York for the funeral, a shake of the head, narrowed, sharp eyes, and not a word spoken.

4

"Roberta," Feng-qi began, when he finally reached his mother-in-law after three days of unreturned messages, although he'd never before addressed her this way, using her given name, and he was suddenly not even sure it *was* her name, it was simply the name he and Maddie had used to refer to her mother, a code, like saying "Madame X" or "the Wicked Witch," and now he was more unsure of himself than when he'd picked up the phone to call, with his prepared script in hand, in two languages so there'd be no slip-up. "I mean, Mrs. Martin—we need your help."

It wasn't a permanent solution, he knew that, and he knew also that she would never agree to live with them in the condo permanently, but he thought if she could just come down to Washington for a few weeks, lend a hand around the house and look after the boys, help them recover from the shock, then he'd have time to make other arrangements. He would decorate the guest room upstairs the way Maddie had always planned, with curtains and a new bed and maybe its own TV, and they'd find a way to co-exist peacefully, for as long as it took, for Maddie's sake, for the sake of the boys.

She listened. She didn't speak, not a word, not even his name. She had never used his name. "They *are* my daughter's children," she said at last.

"Yes," he said.

"You may bring them to me in New York. Or, better yet, *send* them here."

It was out of the question. They were his children; they were all he had left. He couldn't send Simon and Wesley away, couldn't wrap them up and ship them to New York as if they were merchandise, FedEx overnight delivery, special handling extra. And anyway, listening to her voice, the stiff, distant words that betrayed no longing, no emotion, no *life*, he didn't want the boys anywhere near her, didn't want her bitterness to sully their memory of Maddie. Or his.

5

There was one last option.

Arranging the visa for his father wasn't easy. The old man had grown up in Jiangsu Province, in a village near Nanjing, the son of peasants, and though he'd settled in Shanghai after the war and had on occasion since then visited Beijing and, once, Chongqing, he knew nothing of passports, of world travel and its impediments, spoke no English, and everything about the process was, Feng-qi knew, a mystery. The officer in the consulate in Shanghai was sympathetic, even helpful when Feng-qi was able to reach him by telephone, but still it took time. And his father's relocating halfway around the world by himself seemed out of the question; Feng-qi imagined him perpetually roaming the San Francisco airport, if he made it even that far, endlessly searching for a way out, trying to make his Shanghai dialect understood, growing ever more frantic until, like one of the hapless cartoon characters Feng-qi had watched with his sons, his head exploded into a fuming mushroom cloud.

The boys weren't sure they wanted to go with Feng-qi to China to pick up their grandpa, whom they'd never met. Over his usual breakfast of Frosted Flakes, Simon listed the reasons he couldn't go, ticking them off on his pudgy fingers: he'd miss school, swimming lessons, and Liam Nickerson's birthday party, not to mention *Arthur* and *Dragon Tales* on TV. Wesley's objection was more basic: he didn't want to leave his room. Both boys argued that someone had to stay home in case their mother came back. "People come back, sometimes," Simon insisted. "They told us so in church." But Feng-qi arranged more time off from work, talked to Simon's teacher, dipped into savings, booked a cheap flight. It would be fun, he cajoled, a real vacation, almost like Disneyland, plus the boys' first time on an airplane, their first visit to his old home, meeting cousins and great uncles and aunts they didn't even know they had. An adventure. They'd love it. He promised.

6

He hadn't been back to China since he left for school, not even when his mother died—money was tight then, he'd just started working for the government, he and Maddie lived in a one-bedroom garden apartment, Wesley was due, and there was no guarantee that his old activism wouldn't land him in jail the minute he set foot in the People's Republic. Things were different now, looser; probably no one knew his old politics, or cared. That was a lifetime ago, and far away, and this was the *new* new China. Still, stepping off the plane, he looked warily around him: at the police and armed guards who seemed to be everywhere, at immigration and customs clerks, at the sea of Chinese faces surging and jostling past him, and wondered if they knew, wondered if his name was on a list, wondered if he'd made a mistake.

He barely recognized the place. The Shanghai airport was unfamiliar, glittering and efficient, it even *smelled* clean, and then he realized he wasn't in the old terminal, the one he'd left from years before, that they'd built a new international airport in Pu Dong, across the river from the city, an area that not so long ago, at the time he left for the States, was dirt roads and villages and pig farms, and now was laced with elevated superhighways, and buried under concrete and steel, with construction cranes everywhere he looked. Gone were the dark gray streets filled with sturdy, bell-ringing bicycles, replaced by broad avenues and honking cars; gone, too, were the fierce political billboards, overtaken by neon Coca-Cola signs and Golden Arches. Nothing was the same. As a boy, Feng-qi's home was in a *longtang* district, a traditional courtyard house accessible only down a narrow lane just wide enough for the man-powered carts that delivered vegetables and carried away what little trash the family wasn't able to put to some purpose. Not that they had the house to themselves. The Cultural Revolution had left them relatively unscathed, but poverty and overcrowding had not, and four families shared the space originally meant for one.

Not long after Feng-qi left for California, the old house was demolished in a spasm of urban renewal. His parents, and the other families they had lived with so intimately, had been relocated to blocks of dusty, barren flats. Their new home came with no more room than before and a dark, trash-strewn stairwell, but offered a little privacy, at least, and an indoor toilet. His father still lived in that same flat, alone since the death of Feng-qi's mother, without much to show for a life of back-breaking work.

The reunion was awkward, father and son uncomfortable in their embrace, Wesley and Simon hanging back, frightened by the old man, put off by his wispy beard, maybe, or the peculiar sweet bean treats he conjured from his pockets, perplexed by his odd speech.

The boys weren't interested in touring Shanghai, although Feng-qi tried to spark their curiosity. He initiated a walk along the Bund (they liked the boats on the river, but not the way people stared at them, even twisting their necks as they passed by) and through the Old City, up and down the crowded pedestrian mall on Nanjing Road. They didn't appreciate the connection to the name of their building back home in D.C., Nanking Mansion, or absorb his explanation of why it was really the same word, Southern Capital, like Beijing and Peking were both Northern Capital, and he stopped himself when he started to describe the Japanese horrors committed in the capture of Nanjing. He'd been teaching them Chinese since they were old enough to talk, and they knew a few phrases of Mandarin, *ni hao ma*, *wo ai ni*, but they hadn't been drawn to writing or reading Chinese characters, and the related meanings of these names, still strange to two American boys, was too much. The one thing about Shanghai that did excite them was the TV tower that looked like a spaceship on a launch pad, a rocket in the middle of a skyscraper forest. But when they rose to the observation deck and looked out over the city, all they could see was gray fog and a distant glass tower poking its head above a low cloud.

When his father's meager belongings had been packed for shipment or given away to neighbors, Feng-qi watched the old man shuffle through his home one last time, bowing his goodbyes to the walls and to the smoke-blackened ghost of the family shrine that had moved from the old house to the apartment, and would now travel to America.

They made their way back to the airport. Feng-qi's father carried a cloth suitcase under one arm and gripped Simon's hand with the other, chattering to him in Chinese while the boy watched his grandfather's face and nodded, understanding nothing; Wesley ran circles around them all as Feng-qi piled luggage onto a cart; and all four pushed through the automatic doors into the bustling marble-floored hall. After Feng-qi corralled the boys long enough to get them past security, he settled them with his father into a row of hard seats, near a window so Simon and Wesley could watch the planes, and wished Maddie and his mother could see how the old man seemed to glow in the presence of his grandsons. He went off in search of supplies for the trip—water, snacks, a Chinese magazine for his father—and when he returned, with the children nowhere in sight and the old man gazing out the window, lost and bewildered, the glow faded, Feng-qi wondered if there was any hope that this would work. Why had Maddie left him?

7

The condo had seemed spacious when Maddie was there to instill order. Dishes were always washed, wiped dry and returned to the cupboard; books found their way back to shelves, and magazines reposed in neat stacks beneath an end table in the living room, or were carted out to the recycling bin. The boys kept their room reasonably tidy, too, considering their ages, under threat of TV restrictions. But without her discipline—her father had been ex-Navy and then a Wall Street investment banker who had taught her the value of both hierarchy and hard work—the housekeeping floundered, and each room began to close in. Although Feng-qi washed dishes after breakfast and dinner, he left them to dry and accumulate in the drainer. He wasn't sure exactly where the recycling bin was, and it seemed important not to put old magazines in the trash. Now copies of *Time* and *The Economist* proliferated on the coffee table and desk, and stacks of *Vogue* and *Bon Appétit*—they'd been Maddie's subscriptions that Feng-qi had not been able to bring himself to cancel—leaned precariously against the wall behind the couch, leading Feng-qi to impose a new walk-softly rule in the living room to prevent toppling. He wasn't reading any books these days, but somehow the books Maddie had loved and read constantly, novels by Henry James and Jane Austen that still carried Maddie's scent, bloomed unexpectedly, like forgotten tulip bulbs, on every flat surface in the house.

And the boys' room had become a disaster area, not just a minefield but a ravaged landscape of collapsed Lego constructions, shoe-and-sock rubble, and stricken action figures. Feng-qi stopped going in there altogether, except when absolutely necessary: to roust the boys for breakfast each morning, to collect their dirty clothes, to change the bed linens, and, as Maddie had done each night, to read to them at bedtime.

He'd done nothing to remedy the household situation before leaving to bring his father home. So when they walked in the door, weary after the interminable flight from China, the unrelenting disorder was a cruel reminder that his wife was dead.

8

Feng-qi looked at the kitchen clock, the second hand laboring above his father's head while the old man bent over the sink, rinsing tea cups, softly humming. He'd been living with them for a month, during which a routine had haltingly emerged, Feng-qi had gone back to work, and the boys, while still prone to bouts of melancholy when one of them suddenly remembered that *she* was gone, had adjusted. Order, although not fully restored, was now at least an attainable goal. His father had turned out to be a fine cook, assembling surprising stir-fry feasts from the shriveled produce available in the tiny Oriental Market on H Street. The boys seemed to realize that this was an improvement over Feng-qi's repertoire of grilled-cheese sandwiches and delivered pizza, as comforting and reliable as those meals had been. Maddie's subscriptions stopped coming—Feng-qi wasn't sure how his father had arranged that since his English was still limited to what was in the beginning readers Simon brought home from school and what he was learning from the boys—and gradually the flood of his own magazines receded.

9

The boys were in their room. Feng-qi could hear the ping and blip of a video game, their laughter, the hissing electronic explosions of intercepted asteroids, or aliens, or street thugs. They hadn't noticed the time. Feng-qi's father seemed in no hurry, either, but the movie would be starting, cartoon dinosaurs wouldn't wait, and the boys would be upset. There'd be tantrums and accusations. And Jessica Lee would see it all.

But she was late, too. He wanted a quiet hour or two with her, just to talk, to get to know one another, nothing more than that. He didn't want to replace his wife; it was just that he was lonely, and Jessica had been sympathetic in the bookstore when he told her about Maddie, and, maybe, by the time his father and the boys came back from the theater, he and Jessica would be gone, taking a walk down toward the Capitol, or bracing themselves against the wind over the reflecting pool. Or maybe he was ready to introduce her to the boys, to measure their reaction, even though it really was too soon, and he didn't want to scare her. Maybe they'd just sit and wait, sipping coffee, because she was actually American, third generation, had never even been to China, and would prefer coffee; or maybe she'd like to try the Long Jing tea he'd just found in the tea shop in Chinatown, or maybe a beer, or a glass of wine, except Feng-qi didn't think he had any wine in the house. When his father came back there would be surprise and the kind of awkward foot-shuffling that comes with not knowing what to say: the boys would be confused and resentful, if they even had a sense of what it meant that he was seeing this woman, not that it was a date, not really, and they'd sulk in their room; his father would be flustered by this new presence, a Chinese face that didn't speak Chinese, and he'd try to use the English he'd learned, but Jessica wouldn't understand his accent, and little would be said. It would be a disaster, and he'd retrieve her coat from the closet and walk her to the door, stand apologetically with her on the street until she broke away and turned at the corner to wave goodbye.

Finally Feng-qi's father turned off the water and settled the cups in the rack. He wiped his hands on a dishtowel and draped it through the stove handle. He glanced up at the clock, clapped his hands together.

"Tsai-mon," he called. "Wess-lee. Come. We late." He reached into the closet and pulled out the boys' jackets. The laughter from upstairs rose and Feng-qi's father smiled helplessly. "*Kuai-le*," he shouted. Hurry.

The buzzer rang. Sometimes one of his neighbors buzzed, having locked themselves out of the building; sometimes the FedEx driver would press all the buttons, looking for anyone to open the door so he could slip a package inside instead of leaving it on the stoop where it was sure to disappear; sometimes, or so Maddie had explained to the boys, warning them never to open the door unless they knew who they were letting in, a thief would try to gain access to the apartments, where there were fancy stereos and jewelry and other goodies. The buzzer rang again.

Feng-qi shook his head. Jessica had arrived, the boys were still there, and now he'd have to make introductions, the atmosphere all wrong, not what Feng-qi had planned. The boys would miss the movie, they'd whine, she'd think they were spoiled. She was supposed to meet them after, if at all, when everyone was happy and relaxed, open to new possibilities. Not before. He should have hurried them out. He should have insisted that they listen to their grandfather. They *were* spoiled. The buzzer rang again and he pressed the button on the intercom.

"Just a minute," he said. Jessica would not be offended by this small rudeness, would she? She was a kind person; she would understand what can happen in a house full of people, especially when young boys were involved.

The boys thudded down the stairs. The buzzer rang yet again and the boys looked expectantly at the intercom. Feng-qi's father also looked at the intercom and then at Feng-qi.

"Off you go," said Feng-qi, squeezing Simon into his jacket while his father helped Wesley. The buzzer buzzed again.

Then the phone rang.

"*Aiya,*" muttered Feng-qi. He picked up the phone. "*Wei,*" he said, anxiety transporting him back to China, erasing three-quarters of a decade of American customs, and his English. "Hello," he said, remembering where he was. It was Jessica, she was running late, maybe they should just meet somewhere halfway between her apartment and his? At the Starbucks at 7th and H? He set the phone down. The buzzer rang yet again, a long insistent squawk. But now he knew it wasn't Jessica. He pressed the intercom button.

"Hello?"

Feng-qi's father opened the apartment door and shooed the boys into the hall, but they all turned back and watched Feng-qi, speaking to the intercom.

"Fe . . . Mr. Zhang?"

"Yes. Who is it?"

"Roberta Martin. Madeline's mother."

Not Jessica, but Mrs. Martin, the last person Feng-qi would have guessed. Why now? He buzzed her in.

Anticipating the confrontation with Maddie's mother, he joined his father and the boys in the Gallery and nudged each one toward the front, first Simon, then Wesley, then his father. Feng-qi looked for an escape that wasn't there, resigned himself to the confusion he knew was coming. He could already see her through the glass door, still outside on the steps in a long, gray coat, her gray hair swirling in the wind like a cloud, her gray-gloved hand on the door, pressing the buzzer yet again, the yellow glow of a taxi behind her. He'd left the apartment door open and the buzz projected into the Gallery, amplified, echoing, painfully loud. She noticed them now, coming toward her, her face pressed against the glass to see inside, and she mercifully lifted her finger off the buzzer.

At the door, Simon and Wesley huddled behind their grandfather, only their heads poking out on either side of the old man. Mrs. Martin's gaze sought out the boys. Except at the funeral, from a distance, she had never seen Wesley, and had only known Simon briefly as an infant, when Maddie still had hope of bringing her mother into their lives. After that, Maddie spoke to her on the phone occasionally, always initiating the calls, always reporting to Feng-qi that nothing had changed. Maddie had given up, saddened by her mother's rigidness, by the avoidable emptiness in their lives. Feng-qi hadn't cared, not for himself, happy in the snug world they'd created together, but knew from the way Maddie burrowed close to him in bed after a call from her mother that she was deeply wounded.

So he knew Simon and Wesley had no idea who this woman might be, except they'd heard the voice on the intercom say, "Madeline's mother," and they would know who Madeline was. And his father may or may not have understood what had been said. Feng-qi now couldn't remember what he and Maddie had told the boys about her mother, other than that she lived far away. He wasn't sure what to tell them now.

"Boys, this is your grandmother," Feng-qi said slowly when, after a moment's hesitation, Mrs. Martin came through the door he'd opened for her. "Mrs. Martin, this is Simon." He pulled Simon out from behind his grandfather. "And this is Wesley." Wesley came out on his own, bowed stiffly, and then slipped behind his grandfather's legs again. "And my father, Zhang Jian-ping. Dad, this is Maddie's mother, Mrs. Martin." He repeated the introduction in Chinese. His father nodded gravely.

Feng-qi looked at his watch and wondered if he had time to call Jessica before she left for Starbucks. He pictured himself running the three blocks to the shop, arriving breathless, foolish. If he didn't leave right that minute, she'd be sitting in the coffee shop by herself, waiting. Not the impression he wanted to make.

"Mrs. Martin, you've caught us at a bad time, I'm afraid. My father and the boys are going to a movie and I . . . I have an appointment. I'm late, in fact."

"I see," she said. "I suppose I should have called."

Feng-qi looked at his watch again. "It's just that . . ."

"I took the train. I've never liked Washington." Feng-qi saw that the door of the taxi was still open, the engine running, exhaust chuffing out the rear.

A door opened down the hall, and out came Craig and Charles, or Charles and Craig, with their waddling pug Sascha. The men, who had been friendly with Maddie, and had cried loudly at her funeral, both waved, studying the curious crowd at the door.

"Sascha," shouted Simon. The boys ran to the dog, who twisted his leash around Craig's ankle. Or Charles's ankle.

"Sha-sha," shouted Wesley.

Another door opened, and there was Boris, the sculptor. A cigarette hung from his mouth, a knife in his hand. Dry clay streaked his bare chest.

"Heard the commotion," he said. His cigarette filled the Gallery with smoke.

The barefoot painter, whose name Feng-qi suddenly could not remember, opened his door and stepped out, carrying the oily smell of paint with him.

There was a pounding on the glass door. Mrs. Martin jumped, and all turned to see Sam Artoyen, the building's developer, with a young couple in jeans and matching camouflage t-shirts behind him. No one moved. Sam knocked again, and Boris pushed the door open. Sam and the couple came in and Feng-qi grabbed his father's elbow and maneuvered closer to the door.

"*Zou ba,*" said Feng-qi's father. Let's go. Simon and

Wesley gave Sascha a last pat and hurried to their grandfather. The dog yipped.

Cold air rushed inside. A man in a trench coat appeared on the sidewalk and ran up the steps, Feng-qi's boss, Harold.

"Mrs. Martin, would you like to rest in the apartment? I do have this appointment, as I mentioned. I should be back in an hour. Two hours."

"You called me," Mrs. Martin said. "I've booked a suite at the Mayflower. I've come for the children."

"Frank, I'm glad I caught you," said Harold. He balanced a briefcase on his thigh, opened the lid and extracted a folder.

Feng-qi gaped at Maddie's mother.

Sam Artoyen was showing the empty apartment to the newcomers, leaving the door open. Their footsteps on the hardwood floors echoed through the Gallery. The young couple from the front apartment emerged, the man's arm around his wife's shoulders, the sweet fragrance that Feng-qi noticed often accompanied them wafting behind. Harold thrust the folder into Feng-qi's hands. Mrs. Martin looked out toward the taxi.

"We should be going," she said. "You can send their things." She looked at the boys and stepped toward the door.

Feng-qi looked at his watch again.

10

And so they are all here, and Jessica is waiting. Feng-qi can't leave, not now that he understands why Maddie's mother has come, and maybe that is for the best. He feels he should introduce his neighbors and his boss and Mrs. Martin, but there are too many people, too much commotion.

"It's what you wanted," she says.

"No," Feng-qi says, or thinks he says.

"It is December 13," his father says in Chinese.

Feng-qi looks at him. He knows the date and isn't sure why his father should mention it now. Everyone else stares at Feng-qi, waiting for a translation. "The date . . ." he says.

"December 13," his father says again, "the day of the massacre."

"What's he saying?" someone asks.

"Thirty ten-thousands killed by the Japanese barbarians," says Feng-qi's father.

"Is he all right?" Mrs. Martin asks. "He seems upset about something."

Feng-qi no longer understands what anyone is saying. He has been concentrating on his father, who does in fact seem agitated, and only now notices that Jessica has appeared in the doorway. Behind her is Mrs. Martin's taxi-driver, a bulky suitcase straining each arm. He is a small man, dark-skinned, with wavy black hair.

"Lady," the driver says to Mrs. Martin, "are you staying or what?"

"Devils," says Feng-qi's father, speaking, Feng-qi believes, of the Japanese soldiers who killed his father's parents, and neighbors, and friends.

"When you didn't show up, I thought I'd just come over," Jessica says, looking from Feng-qi to his father, to his boys, to Mrs. Martin, to Boris, to Sam Artoyen and his clients, to the painter, to Charles and Craig and Sascha, to the arm-linked couple. "But maybe now's not a good time." She moves toward the door.

"Papa, we'll miss the movie," Simon whines and tugs on his father's sleeve.

"Put those back in the cab," Mrs. Martin says to the taxi-driver, who shrugs, despite the heavy bags. Now it seems that everyone is speaking at once and Feng-qi isn't sure who is saying what to whom. He believes he hears Maddie laughing, and he turns to look for her, but all he sees is the open door to their apartment.

"Wait!" he shouts.

Feng-qi never shouts. The Gallery falls silent. The boys huddle close together, eyes wide.

Boris is shaking his head as he slips back into his apartment, his cigarette smoke lingering. Harold leaves, pointing at the folder in Feng-qi's hands as he backs through the door. Charles and Craig, with tiny waves, head outside, clipping Sascha's leash to his collar. Sam Artoyen ushers the prospective buyers through the diminishing crowd and out onto the stoop. He, too, waves, as he shows the couple to their Jetta, parked in front of the fire hydrant. The painter disappears. The young couple, perhaps forgetting they were on their way out, head back into their apartment, arm in arm.

Feng-qi steps forward, takes the suitcases from the taxi-driver and sets them down in the Gallery. He pays the driver, who stuffs the bills in his shirt pocket, and shrugs again before climbing back into his cab.

Simon edges toward Mrs. Martin and looks up at her. She clutches her purse. Feng-qi thinks he sees her hands shaking when she bends slightly and gazes down at Simon.

"Are you my grandma?" the boy asks.

She nods. He reaches up, pries one arm from her purse, and takes her hand.

Feng-qi places his hand on Mrs. Martin's elbow and, as she casts a glance over her shoulder toward her luggage, he guides her through the Gallery and into the apartment. His father and the boys follow. Then Jessica. The apartment door remains open, the Gallery oddly vacant and quiet.

He arranges the women on the couch in the living room, Mrs. Martin at one end, Jessica at the other, and in the kitchen boils water for tea. From where he stands, contemplating the next move, wondering how this could end any way but badly, he sees the boys run upstairs and then run back down, each with a stuffed animal in his hand, Wesley's panda, Simon's dragon. They settle cautiously on either side of their grandmother, dropping the animals in her lap.

Feng-qi's father stands at the bottom of the stairs, his eyes on Feng-qi. "My family," says the old man, in Chinese. "December 13."

"He's trying to say something," says Mrs. Martin.

What he's saying, Feng-qi realizes, is that this is the day of the attack on Nanjing, the day the world changed, the day Feng-qi's own grandparents were slaughtered by the Japanese, the day hundreds of thousands of Chinese died, the day thousands of families were destroyed. Should Feng-qi say something to his father? Is it comfort he wants?

Jessica sits stiffly on her hands, twisting to look at the open door, apparently not sure whether to stay, or go, to fill the silence, or to remain mute. Or is she wondering if there is a place for her here in this family? Feng-qi watches Mrs. Martin's eyes move from the scrolls of Chinese calligraphy in the dining area, to the fragile altar his father has recreated in a corner of the living room, with a faded sepia photograph of a young Chinese couple, a precarious pyramid of oranges, a framed picture of Feng-qi's mother, one of Maddie, and one half-burned stick of incense. The kettle shrieks. Feng-qi sprinkles green tea leaves into four mugs and pours in the water. He places the mugs on a lacquered tray and carries them to the living room. Mrs. Martin sits erect, waiting. Her gaze returns to the altar. He sets the tray on the coffee table and moves one mug to a coaster in front of her, and one in front of Jessica. He picks up one for himself and sits across from the women. Mrs. Martin stares into the mug of tea, steam rising, the dark leaves still floating and swirling on the surface, and then again at the altar. Feng-qi knows he should offer to replace the tea with something else, an English tea, in a bag, maybe with milk and sugar. But he doesn't. This is his tea, his Chinese tea. She replaces her cup on the tray and puts an arm around each of the boys, pulls them closer when they squirm away.

Feng-qi puts down his mug. He glances at his father, who is standing before his altar, eyes shut, hands clasped at his chest. Feng-qi slips out and brings Mrs. Martin's luggage inside the apartment, positioning the suitcases at the foot of the stairs. He peers into the empty Gallery at the abstract paintings.

He closes the door.

A HOLE IN THE WALL

Aloysius wields the sledge hammer like a baseball bat, banging a crater into the drywall. He swings it a second time, up, like a golf club, then down, then like a bat again. He pictures a face on the wall, his ex-boss at his ex-law firm, and obliterates it with a dead-on swing. The room shakes, white chunks land at his feet, dust fills his nose and clings to his glasses.

He pulls the drywall away, expecting to find insulation underneath, and exposes bare brick instead. He lifts the hammer again, sees a face in the mottled brick he takes to be his father's, features he has only imagined on a man he's never known, and swings again. He pictures Erika, his soon-to-be-ex-wife, her profile in the cracked mortar, and blasts a hole in the wall. It shouldn't be this easy, but it is. Air and light rush in. Bricks clack down three stories to the alley pavement.

He had purchased the tri-level condo directly from the developer after he and Erika split. In a corner of the Lower Shaw neighborhood, a multi-racial enclave on the rise, it was a steal, and he's beginning to understand why. He had had big plans for the place: a bright kitchen with gleaming new appliances, an expanded bathroom in the basement, a balcony upstairs, off the master bedroom. He'd been going to paint the dining room—he had a pale green in mind, the same color his mother's had been, not that he harbored fond memories of that house—but he'd made it no further than retrieving paint samples from Home Depot. He'd intended to buy all new furniture, a bedroom suite, a sofa and matching armchair, and heard from a colleague at work, a woman whose family had lived in Georgetown for three generations, that Crate & Barrel was a good store. But when he visited their glossy Tysons Corner showroom he was shocked by the prices, and by the platinum-haired saleswoman who as much as told him that a young black man might be more comfortable shopping at Grand's or another discount furniture seller. As a result, he has painted nothing and bought nothing, and still sleeps in a sleeping bag on the floor, cooks on the vintage stove, eats his meals standing up in the dark, drab kitchen.

Although he's lived in Nanking Mansion two months—three?—he's met few neighbors. There's the paint-smeared artist who wouldn't shake his hand and the arm-locked couple who barely glanced at him as he was moving in. At least the girl smiled. And except for the unit next to his, he hasn't been inside any of the other apartments. His cell phone had died and service in the condo hadn't been turned on, so he knocked on his neighbor's door to call Verizon. He'd been admitted by a Chinese man who showed him to the phone, and while he waited to be connected to a human being at the phone company, the man and his two little boys, one a toddler and one not much older, eyed him like wary mice watching a hawk.

Aloysius stares through the hole in his wall. The Washington monument peeks over the trees, and, if he shifts to the right and angles his head just so, he sees the radiant Capitol dome. He moves closer, his head nearly inside the hole, as if tempting a lion, and looks down into the alley, with its drifts of Styrofoam peanuts, wind-strewn leaves, yellowed newspaper, and who-knows-what-manner of urban detritus. This will be his view when the balcony is finished. Simple enough to manage: he'll keep his head high, ignore what lies below. He leans the hammer against the wall, waves the hanging dust cloud from his face, and rests.

The phone rings. He gazes across the room at the machine on the floor, its cord looping to the wall, and lets it ring. He never answers the phone, a habit he learned from Erika, who had screened all their calls, never anxious to speak to her hypochondriac mother or, worse, *his* mother. She, invariably, would be looking for drugs or money to buy drugs, and Erika had no sympathy. When the ringing stops he hears his own voice, tinny and distant: "This is Aloysius. Just Aloysius. No one else. Please leave a message. For Aloysius." The machine beeps, and he waits, but there is only silence and a dead click.

As he always does when this happens, he runs through a list of who might have been calling. His office? Not likely. There are dedicated souls at his new firm, O'Fallon & Goldstein, government regulatory lawyers who work late during the week and even put in full days on Saturdays. He's one of them. But on a Sunday afternoon, other than Mr. O'Fallon himself, the place is deserted. The saner workload had been one of its attractions, and reason number two (right behind his maniacal boss) for leaving his old firm. His wife? Estranged-wife, he corrects himself. Erika only calls to chastise him for some perceived slight, or to crow over the publication of her latest article, or an award she's received. His sister? Also not likely. Although she lives just a few miles away, down in their old Anacostia neighborhood, he and Gwen haven't spoken to each other in at least three years, not since she got on his case for dating a white woman and then refused to attend their wedding. He hasn't called to tell her about the separation, won't give her the satisfaction. His mother? He hopes not. He can't help her. With any kind of luck, his mother's dead.

It's a short list, not a happy one.

The sky is darkening outside the hole. He smells the thick, acrid odor of new tar—from the alley, or New York Avenue, or where?—and realizes how foolish he's been. What was he thinking? Yes, the work needs to be done, it's where the new balcony must go, and the contractors promised to be on the job first thing Monday. He's arranged the morning off to let them into the building, get them started, and the job should be done by the time he gets home in the evening. But they'll think he's nuts for starting it without them, this lawyer in an empty condo who knows nothing about construction, who found a sledge hammer in the basement and came out swinging. And tonight? There's a fucking hole in the wall. What's he going to do tonight?

He'll have to cover it. He has no plastic sheets, though, no tape, nothing. In his old place, the bungalow he and Erika own in Woodley Park, where she still lives, he'd run out to the corner hardware store for what he needs. But in this edge-of-a-war-zone neighborhood, where even the liquor store is boarded up, that's not an option. He could ask one of the neighbors, the sculptor or the painter, or the Chinese man with the toddlers. One of them might have plastic or tarps. But he still barely knows these people and he's in no mood to knock on doors, to explain himself. He'll have to get in the car, cross the river and find a suburban strip mall, pray that stores are open on a Sunday night, maybe head back to Home Depot.

But he doesn't want to leave the hole. Not because he's drawn to it. Not because holes hold any special meaning for him, although this one does remind him of a painting he admires in the National Gallery, with blue sky and puffy clouds over red brick—is it by Magritte? But it's a fucking hole! Rats could get in. Bats. Or worse. It's a stupid thing to have made, that hole. Stupid.

He paces, hoping for inspiration. He's a practical man, resourceful. He overcame his background, a kid from Southeast D.C., pulled himself up, worked his way through law school. On track for partnership at a prestigious firm as long as he doesn't get distracted. If there's a problem, he can solve it.

When the solution, albeit a temporary one, hits him, he smiles.

He pulls towels from the bathroom cabinet and stuffs them in the hole. It takes three, loosely wadded, to fill the damn thing. Four, counting the one that glides down to the alley like a magic carpet.

When he gets out to the street, list in hand, and sees his Saab in a rare, prime spot right in front of the building, he changes his mind about the plastic and tape. He's filled the hole. It'll be fine. The contractors will come in the morning. He'll feel foolish, but he'll comfort himself by believing they've seen worse. Trash fires gone wild. Plumbing jobs turned flood. A hole isn't so bad. He can live with the hole for one night.

The first thing he sees in the morning is light slipping through gaps between towels and brick. But sleep has eased the sting of embarrassment and he doesn't feel quite as dumb as he did last night. The wall will be fixed today, by professionals, and no one will ever know. It's not like it will hurt his chance to make partner. He won't tell a soul. Or he might tell Erika, as a gift, something for her to feel superior about.

His brief foray into therapy had taught him that his residual fondness for Erika was normal. Besides, as he'd explained to his divorce lawyer, he's not convinced their differences are truly irreconcilable. They used to communicate and now they don't. Something's gone missing. The fact that she wanted kids and he didn't was only part of the story. But irreconcilable? Erika may think so. He's not so sure.

He makes coffee. He stands at the kitchen counter eating a piece of toast, catching crumbs in his hand. The phone rings, too early for the usual suspects, and he considers answering it. But the machine picks up, and after his own voice, he hears the tentative stammer of the contractor.

"Um, Mr. Penn? This is Gordon Johnson from, um, Johnson Construction and I'm afraid we aren't going to get out to your place today. If you could give us a call so we can reschedule . . . um, anyway. Thanks."

Stupid. He's going to have to live with the hole another day. At least. Stupid.

At Home Depot, he has tape and a plastic tarp in his hands when he wonders if the tape will stick to brick. He considers asking one of the clerks, but in his experience they're all know-nothing amateurs, and, anyway, he doesn't want to explain why there's a hole in his wall. Even an amateur would realize how foolish he's been. If the tape works, fine. If not, he still has the towels.

Back home, when he pulls the towels out of the hole, another brick comes loose and drops into the alley. Stupid. He edges his head outside and is relieved that the brick hasn't clobbered anyone. When he's about to take measurements so that the plastic will be just the right size, pleased with himself that he's taking action to deal with his problem, he notices the light blinking on the answering machine. It holds him motionless. He puts down the plastic, moves to the phone, and presses play.

"Al, it's Gwen. Long time, huh? Listen, little brother, got your number from the white bitch. You know how much I loved *that* conversation. Al, honey, you didn't even tell me 'bout you two. Didn't give your own sister your new address. But that's not why I called. Got some news. You've got my number."

He wishes she'd just left the news in the message. Why

couldn't she do that? It's what answering machines are for, especially when people aren't speaking to each other. And that's not just because of Erika. Gwen had started down the same road as their mother, once upon a time. She'd cleaned up and slipped. Cleaned up and slipped again. He's been happy thinking of himself as an orphaned, only child. It suits him. He doesn't want her in his life, and now he'll have to call her. But not this minute. Right now, he has other problems.

He hears a faint knocking and realizes someone is at the door to his apartment. He takes a step, stops. The hole that he doesn't want to leave untended tugs at him, but there's the knocking again, louder, longer. He hurries downstairs.

It's his Chinese neighbor, with both of the boys huddled behind. Aloysius remembers now, there'd been a wife—a white wife—the building's developer had told him. They had that in common. She's gone now. Dead. He tries to remember how.

"Yes?"

"No school today," says the Chinese man. Is his name Funchy? No, but something like that, unfamiliar, unpronounceable.

"School?"

"The boys. No school today. I have work. I hear you. From next door." He points. Aloysius begins to explain about the hole, but stops. He nods.

"You can watch the boys?" The man looks at his watch. "Until afternoon?"

He wants to protest. There's no way he can do this, but suddenly the man is gone and the boys are inside his apartment, staring at him. What kind of man leaves his children with a total stranger? Not total, maybe, but still. Is that what they do in China?

He asks questions—why is there no school, who usually looks after them, what are their names, is the little one even old enough for school?—but the boys have no answers. He thinks they speak English—he recalls hearing them shout in the hallway and surely it was English he'd heard—but perhaps they don't understand what he's asked. And it now occurs to him that he has only arranged for the morning off, that he'll need to call his office.

He remembers the hole. He directs the boys through the apartment toward the steps. They exchange glances when they see he has no furniture, which he supposes must seem odd to them. It *is* odd. Up they go and at the top of the stairs there is a breeze and a round stream of light, like a spotlight, pouring through the hole.

"Whoa," says the older boy. "There's a hole in the wall." The boys run to examine it.

The three of them stand before the wall, the light shining on the boys' faces, and there is a simultaneous flutter and coo as a pigeon alights on the edge of the hole.

"Cool," says the older boy.

He explains to the boys the project he has in mind for covering the hole, but they don't seem interested. The older boy—he finally tells Aloysius that his name is Simon and his brother's name is Wesley—has been chewing gum and he now takes the wad from his mouth and throws it at the pigeon, who ducks but is otherwise unperturbed.

The phone rings and Aloysius listens for a message.

"It's me," says Erika's voice. "Your delightful sister is looking for you. Thought you'd want to know." Her tone is soft, gracious, not at all the meanness she's capable of. She knows, he knows, that his sister's call probably isn't welcome, good news or bad. Erika's a fine woman. Too proud sometimes, combative, but they'd had a good run. Dance clubs, jazz. That woman could move. He closes his eyes.

He opens them and the boys are staring at him again. The pigeon has now landed inside the room, is pecking at the hardwood floor, and there is another roosting in its place in the hole.

The boys laugh and chase the bird, who hops to stay ahead of them. The second bird is now inside, as well, strutting, pecking, cooing. Aloysius isn't as disturbed by this intrusion as he thinks he would be if the kids weren't there. For them it's grand entertainment, and watching them chase the birds—they've split up now that the little one has his own bird to torment—is entertainment for him.

The phone rings again. This time they all turn to look at the machine. Even the birds seem to stop, to wait for the jangling interruption to end.

"Shit." It's Gwen's voice. "I know you're there. I called your damn office, so you better pick up the damn phone."

He studies the faces of the boys to see if they react to the profanity. Their eyes are wide, but he suspects they're more shocked by Gwen's angry tone than by the actual language which they've possibly never heard. She's bitter, her voice is like breaking glass, and just as sharp. She sounds sober, though, so that's a plus.

The boys go back to chasing the pigeons. It occurs to Aloysius that if they join forces, the three of them might be able to drive the birds toward the hole and, with luck, the flying rats might find their way out before he has globs of birdshit all over the floor. He explains to the boys what he wants to do and they nod eagerly. All three move to the wall farthest from the hole, slide gingerly past the pigeons and join hands. They step forward together and the birds hop away, nearing the hole. They step again and the birds move again. They step a third time but the little one, Wesley, gets too excited and kicks at the birds, who launch into flight, one passing under the trio's linked arms, one passing over. They start again, slowly, and this time they succeed in maneuvering the birds close to the hole. Do they smell the fresh air? Do they see the sky? Do they sense that just through that bright opening are more of their kind? Another step forward and one of the birds takes off and disappears out the hole. The second bird looks confused, suddenly alone with these strangers. The three step forward again and now this one is gone, too. Aloysius cheers and the boys join him.

They help him pile the towels back into the hole. Then Simon says, "We're hungry." Aloysius doesn't have much food in the house, but he puts bread in the toaster and locates margarine, cinnamon and sugar, with which he concocts two slices of cinnamon toast. He has no milk, but he does have orange juice. He drinks coffee and the three of them have a makeshift picnic on the floor of the cavernous living room.

After their success herding pigeons, the boys seem more comfortable with him and they answer questions. Simon is in kindergarten, Wesley in pre-school. But not today. They aren't sure why not today. Aloysius knows the mother is gone, but he hesitates to ask about her. He doesn't have to.

"Our mother is dead," says Simon. "She had an accident."

"But she's coming back," says Wesley. He says it with confidence, as if repeating words he has learned, but then looks at his big brother. He tilts his head, eyes welling. "Isn't she?"

Simon nods, but in his eyes Aloysius sees understanding, a depth of awareness that he recognizes and is sure the boy won't articulate. And Aloysius knows, too, that they *don't* come back. Even when they're not dead. They walk out, they don't say goodbye, and they're never heard from again. They leave a void, and that void never gets filled.

Snack time over, they return to the hole. With the help of Simon—while Wesley watches, distracted by a strip of duct tape Aloysius has given him—he unrolls the plastic, measures a square, cuts, and tapes it over the hole. The tape adheres to the brick better than he expects and the plastic holds firm. They stand back to admire their work, Simon's hands on his hips in imitation of Aloysius.

Wesley has managed to stick his strip of tape on his hair and is struggling to get it off. Aloysius kneels at the boy's side and tugs on the tape, but all he does is pull Wesley's hair. The boy shrieks and emits a string of choking sobs, on the threshold of a wall-piercing wail. Aloysius picks him up, holds him in his arms, and the sobs subside. Downstairs he tries again to pull the tape free, gently this time, but it doesn't budge. Erika would know what to do, he realizes. She's good with kids. He's seen her with her sister's brood. But he's clueless. There are scissors in the utility drawer in the kitchen and with a warning to Wesley to sit still, that scissors are sharp and dangerous and should be handled carefully—advice he has no recollection of having received when he was a child—he cuts the tape free, along with a substantial clump of Wesley's dark-but-not-quite-black hair. Simon laughs when he sees it. Aloysius laughs, too, and hopes this won't start Wesley crying again, so he picks the boy up one more time and carries him into the downstairs bathroom, showing him the jagged mess that is the side of his head. And now Wesley laughs.

The morning has passed. Aloysius looks at his watch twice because he can't quite believe it. He allows himself to admit that he's enjoyed being with the boys and wonders what would have happened if he and Erika had had children after all. Would they still be together? Would that have been enough? Or would it have snuffed whatever spark they'd felt? Would life now just be even more miserable and complicated while they battled over custody and money, and ruined their children's lives as well as their own?

There's nothing else in the house to eat, but he pours more juice. He shows them how to wash the glasses, although this is something they already seem to know, even Wesley, whom Aloysius has perched on a stool—too precariously, he realizes—so the boy can reach the sink. When there's a knock on the door, they all turn their heads.

It's their father, he expects. He's almost sorry that his time with them is over, but he has things to do. He never got around to calling the contractor, or his office. He didn't call Gwen. He doesn't move, and the knock comes again.

When he opens the door, there is the boys' father standing next to Gwen. Aloysius can't speak. How does his Chinese neighbor know his sister? Is this what she was trying to tell him?

Grinning now, the man holds out a bottle. The label is gold, with Chinese writing.

"Thank you. Please take wine. Thank you." The boys' father leaves the bottle in Aloysius's hands and summons Simon and Wesley, who slip past Gwen into the hall. Aloysius wants to explain what happened to Wesley's hair, but it's too late. The boys wave and disappear into their own apartment.

"What were you doing with those China boys, brother? Is there something you ain't telling me?" Gwen's smirk is the customary half-smile, half-sneer he remembers. Her skin is mostly clear, but there are traces of old meth damage on her cheeks, scars that are slow to heal. Her hands rest on her substantial hips. Weight gain is a good sign, he thinks. She smells of cigarettes, though, and as soon as he realizes that's what the odor is, she reaches into her handbag, pulls out a pack and her lighter.

"You and the white girl split?" She strides into the apartment.

"You talked to Erika." He's thinking about the hole upstairs, the thin sheet of plastic that covers it, how fragile it seems.

"I knew it was a mistake."

"So you said."

"But you did it anyway."

"Is that why you're here? To tell me I fucked up? Like you're such a great role model." He looks at his watch, hoping she'll take the hint. He assumes there's news about their mother. Why else would she bother? He folds his arms, waits. But Gwen can't be rushed. When they were kids, she'd known what he wanted or what their mother wanted, and managed to do exactly the opposite. It's a gift. No reason to think she's lost it.

"Not *just* that." She spins around the room, as if looking for a place to sit. She snorts and shakes her head, and stops in the middle of the empty space. She glowers, eyes narrowed. Her nose flares. She lights her cigarette and smoke erupts toward the ceiling.

Aloysius hears the flutter of wings upstairs. The birds are back, despite the plastic. Gwen doesn't seem to notice.

"He came to see me," she says.

It's like the phantom phone calls. Who? He runs through the possibilities, but he knows so little about his sister's life these days that he can barely begin. Gwen's not married, there are no ex-boyfriends he knows about. Ex-dealers maybe. But he's not going to ask. Let Gwen have her drama. He goes to the window and opens it, taking his mind back to the hole upstairs. He expects to see Gwen's smoke rush out, sucked into the ether, maybe her along with it. But it lingers over their heads, like a curse.

"Aren't you going to ask who?"

"No time for games, Gwen."

She holds her cigarette at an angle, its ash precariously long. There are no ash trays, no potted plants. She holds out her palm but appears to reconsider and comes to the window, tossing the cigarette outside into the litter-filled alley. She waves her hands in the air as if she can disperse the cloud she's unleashed. The smoke swirls and the cloud reforms.

He leans back against the wall, hands in his pockets. The fluttering upstairs comforts him. He hears Simon and Wesley laughing in the hallway. They're cooing, imitating the birds.

"All right. You win. Who came to see you?"

Gwen's arms are folded across her chest. "Our father," she says, as if beginning a prayer. Now she looks at *her* watch. "Guess what? He wants to see his boy, and I was only too glad to give him your new address. In fact, if my timing's as lousy as usual I'd say he's due here any minute." She's already at the door when she reaches into her purse and pulls out a business card. "This is him. I've got no use for it." She tosses the card on the bare floor, where it spins on one corner like a top. And she leaves.

From where he stands there is a glare on the card, making it appear radiant, its own source of heat. He knows it's an illusion, like the reflected light of the moon.

He picks it up, tucks it into a pocket, and heads back upstairs. He has calls to make, the day is nearly gone, and he needs to get things under control. As he climbs the stairs he remembers that the pigeons have returned. They coo and flap their wings at his approach. When he gets to the top he sees them, a dozen or more strutting, pecking, looking, searching. A breeze carries the tar scent through the hole and ruffles the dangling tape and plastic where his improvised window has fallen to the floor.

The phone rings. It's the contractor. They want to schedule a time to do the work on his balcony. But now he's having second thoughts about the balcony. The view back there isn't so great, vacant buildings and a trash-strewn alley. It might be dangerous. It might hurt resale value. Prospective buyers who have children wouldn't like it. The whole idea has gone sour.

The phone rings again. After he hears his own recorded words once more, there is a pause.

"Aloysius?" The voice on the machine is rough and hoarse, an abused instrument. He doesn't recognize it, and yet he knows who it is. "Your sister gave me this number. I want to talk to you, son. I was going to drop by, but . . . We've got some catching up to do, you and me. I know . . ." The voice trails off and he thinks the message is over, but then it's back. "Anyway," it says, and leaves a number.

Aloysius asks, as if the pigeons could tell him, "Why

now?" The man has been gone since forever and now, today, when he gets the tiniest taste of what it means to be a father, the asshole shows up. Reminding him what fathers do. They disappear. They beat their wives and their daughters and sons and they sell dope and they walk out. They cause pain. They ruin lives.

He pulls the card from his pocket. There was a time, a long time ago, when he wondered about the man. What he was like. What he did. A very long time ago. He doesn't look at the card, doesn't want to know what it says. He drives the pigeons toward the hole, wishing the boys were there to help. But even alone, weaving in an arc around the birds, he moves them. One by one they find the hole and leave. Until there is only one bird left. The pigeon cocks its head and assesses him, as if taking the measure of this man who has blasted a hole in this wall and forsaken fatherhood. And then it takes flight, into the sky beyond.

He watches the bird soar and disappear into the glint of the sun off the Capitol dome. The card is still in his hand, the telephone just feet away. He thinks of his wife, of the life they had, what could have been. He reaches through the hole in the wall, holds his hand steady, feels the soothing breeze on his arm, and lets the card fall. It flutters and spins and drifts and, finally, comes to rest in the chaos of the world.

THE FACE IN THE WINDOW

It is the middle of the night, a dark, moonless night, when a man—a small man who, though past forty, has never been as fit as he is now, his days filled with running and the endless lifting of makeshift weights—removes a painting from the lobby wall. He intends to be noiseless, but the painting is large, an awkward size that exceeds one man's grasp, and a corner of the canvas bumps the wall.

In the apartment behind the wall, another man stirs in his sleep, not knowing what has disturbed him. The man wakes, listens, tries to focus his hearing, to tune out the city, the distant sirens, the rumble of night traffic on nearby New York Avenue. When there is only silence, no imminent threat he can discern, he drifts back to slumber. In the morning he will not remember that he woke. No one else has heard.

In the lobby, which in reality is just a wide hall shared by the vintage building's twelve condos, the small man maneuvers the painting through an open door and leans it against the wall. He steps back into the center of his apartment, a spacious, open loft, and gazes at the work.

The painting is abstract, but the man knows what it depicts: the rooflines of a barn against a winter-blue sky. A thick, white silo stands just off center. There is a face in the window of the barn, but that might as well be a shadow, reflected light, a smudge, an accident. The man has a hunting knife at the ready, one he has sharpened for this purpose, and he means to shred the painting, to return it from whence it came, to nothingness, his imagination, to eliminate that face, that smudge, that accident. But there's no hurry. The rest of the building sleeps, and so shall he.

The man whose sleep has been disturbed, a young lawyer named Aloysius, now rises, at his usual hour, to the familiar voices of the morning news on his radio, no memory of the midnight thump, and leaves for work at his office on K Street without noticing that the large painting is gone. Likewise, the schoolteacher in Number 1, Craig, half of the gay couple that seems always to be on the verge of calamity, exits his apartment with his arrogant pug for their morning walk. This man pauses in the hall as if aware of an imbalance, a new scent, a change he cannot identify, but shrugs and leaves without further examination. The Chinese man, Mr. Zhang, and his two young sons—sadly, their blond mother has been taken from them in a Beltway accident—emerge from their unit chaotically, ahead of Mr. Zhang's ancient father. The boys race to the front door, the men hurry after them, and no one sees the gap where the painting of the barn—if they had ever stopped to realize it was a barn—once hung.

The small man—his name is Calvin—also rises, but has nowhere to go. In the corner of his apartment that is dedicated to his work, he stares at a blank canvas, imploring a picture to appear. But he sees nothing. There is no image in his mind that will emerge in paint for the world to see, and so all he can do is stare at nothing, as he has been doing now for weeks, maybe months. Nothing new will come; it is finished for him. He has only the bones and blood of the work he has eviscerated, kept like sacred relics, work returned from the galleries, work that will not sell, his life's work that was garbage, and is now garbage. Only the painting of the barn remains, and when that is gone, when there is nothing left of who he was, when he has reduced his existence to dust and ashes, he can be reborn. He can begin again.

He holds the knife aloft, but he cannot bring himself to do the deed. Not yet. It is irreversible, this erasure of the self, and, after all, there is no rush. Whatever lies beyond will still be there tomorrow.

Calvin dresses to run and flees the apartment. He ran also in school, as a boy. He was fast, small and fleet, dazzling, and it pleased him. Not the performing, not the races, not the attention, not being on a team—which he was persuaded would endear him to his fellows who, before that, had taunted him for his stature—but the running itself, being absorbed into his subconscious, without will, an instrument of thoughtless motion, streaking across the landscape like a brush.

And now he runs again because he cannot paint.

He heads down M Street. Despite the presence of urban pioneers, like the residents of his own building, it is still a neighborhood of struggles, of broken families in decline, and his appearance—the bare, white legs, his freckled, gaunt cheeks and red locks—is an oddity. A heavy woman with a toddler in hand stops and they both stare at Calvin as he passes. A bald man, wheelchair-bound, watches from a dark window. But these days when Calvin runs, he doesn't see; he doesn't think or feel, and so he doesn't know that he is watched. He only knows that he must run.

He turns south on 4th Street and disturbs a transaction in the alley, detects voices, words that might be angry, but do not register. Both men in the alley, members of the gang that rules this triangular section of the Lower Shaw neighborhood, have guns tucked into their belts. One of the men is an undercover policeman from the city's anti-gang task force, the other a career thug, but both will die violently, if not today, then on another day like today. They have already vanished from Calvin's awareness as he flies down to Massachusetts, heads east over the freeway, to the Capitol steps, back along the Mall, soaring between monuments and museums, invisible to the tourists he does not see, who feel only a faint wind as he passes.

While he runs, a breeze through an open window of his apartment lifts the barn painting away from the wall. It teeters on the brink of tumbling forward where it would be impaled on the sharp edges of his crude barbell, the one he made with cement-filled coffee cans as a desperate teenager, praying for bulk against his oppressive stepfather. But the breeze subsides, and the canvas settles back against the wall.

The man is gone for hours, or it could be days. Racing past the Lincoln Memorial, he approaches two other runners, Marines detailed to the Pentagon who jog daily across the river into the District, one a head taller than the other. They will both one day fight in Iraq and the taller man will die in a helicopter crash. Each observes Calvin, his powerful stride as he catches them and pulls away, surprising in someone his size, and they are compelled to pursue. He doesn't notice that he has passed them, doesn't realize when they fall off his pace, doesn't miss them when they fade, their energy sapped, and stop, short of breath, in the shadow of the Vietnam wall.

When Calvin returns to Nanking Mansion (his home of two years and a vast improvement over the space he once shared with another painter and that painter's girlfriend), he shuts his eyes to the empty wall that no one else has noticed. But inside his apartment he cannot now tear his eyes from the painting of the barn.

He remembers this work, can still feel the resistance of the canvas to his brush strokes, the shudder of the surface beneath his hand. He'd been invited to a community of artists, a colony in the foothills of the Blue Ridge, and the work flowed in his bright studio. Day after day the work came to him, pouring from images in his mind, through his fingers to the canvas, as if he were only a conduit for a creator he could not name. Meals were served to the artists and he would sometimes eat, sometimes not, because there was work to be done, more work than he could grasp, a universe of work, and he would return to the studio even in the dark to let the pictures come.

He spoke to almost no one there. He was something of a joke among the others, especially the writers, so solemn and dark and oblivious he was that each of them, independently and without sharing the idea, resolved to write about him, to let this odd character emerge in words, this short, silent man with the paint-stained hands. When he did appear at meals they would stare at him, extracting details they might use, the spread of his nose, the squint of his eyes, the shiny trace of a scar on his wrists, and he wouldn't notice them noticing him.

Except for one.

There was a woman who spoke to him, and he painted for her. The pictures came through him because of her. She opened him. It is her face in the window.

He now stands before her, before his portrait of her, stripped of everything, the blissful agony of his run coursing through him. Sweat floods the red thatch on his chest and stomach, cascades off his penis, pools at his feet. He lifts the barbell, curling his sculpted biceps. He lifts again, and again, and again. The veins in his arms swell as he lifts, dark, pulsing strokes against his pale skin. He lifts, his penis engorges, the sweat pours, and he stares at the face in the painting until he can lift no more.

It is the two little boys, Simon and Wesley, the only children in the building, who notice that the painting is gone. When they come in with their grandfather—Simon fresh from school and Wesley from the park where the old gentleman, recently arrived from Shanghai and still unaccustomed to such things, has watched the boy frolic with children of many colors—Simon stops and stares at the vacant wall.

"Where's the big picture?" Simon asks his grandfather.

The old man doesn't understand the words, his English being still rudimentary, but he now sees that the crazy painting that was there is no longer there. He lifts his hand to the outline on the wall, a product of grime and faded paint, and traces with one finger the dozen strokes of the Chinese character "huà," meaning art. When the boys' father comes home from work, the old man tells him in Chinese that the painting is gone.

The men inspect the hallway, note the vacant space, and examine the remaining artwork as if for the first time: a cluttered collage by the tall, skinny sculptor in Number 3 who, at this moment, is cutting clay from a block that will become a bust of his father, distorted and wrinkled in a way the man never was in life; an impressionist piece, provenance unknown, reminiscent of Monet, portraying the Tidal Basin ringed by cherry trees in full blossom; and an insipid watercolor of the Washington Monument surrounded by red blobs that apparently represent American flags, painted by the talentless and amorphous woman in the front apartment, Susanna, who takes inspiration from her loutish boyfriend, to whom she has been devoted since high school, who is always by her side and who has, just now, while the Chinese men studied the hallway gallery, in judgment-clouding ecstasy, not for the first time, ejaculated inside her without protection.

Other residents, just home from work, are notified of the disappearance, although Calvin, who is aware of the commotion in the hallway, does not answer when the knock comes to his door. No one knows, or perhaps no one remembers, that the missing painting is his creation. They knock because he must be warned. Everyone must be warned. Calvin listens to their voices. He lies naked on the floor before his painting and listens, stroking himself, summoning the woman in the window.

There have been thefts from the building in the past. It is, after all, a neighborhood in transition, not the safest in the city, although far from the worst, and all of the investors in the building's renovation have the impression that crime in the area has abated. They are wrong, but no one will tell them so. Craig, the high school English teacher, who fancies himself a poet and reads Whitman every evening, is the current President of the Condo Association, and he checks documents, reviews insurance records. Calls are made, the police notified. Doors are examined for evidence. Residents are questioned.

The knock on Calvin's door is insistent now, but still he does not answer.

He knows the theft has been discovered. Eventually someone will remember that he is the artist. They will realize what has happened. They will guess what the odd little man has done.

In the morning, before he runs, he stands before the painting again, knife in hand. Her name was Sook-ja, small, Korean, a violinist and a poet both. She wanted to be called Sarah, while she was in America, such a short time. Like him, she barely spoke to others in the colony. She came to his studio, she posed, she undressed, they fucked on the daybed, on the floor. He knew this wasn't how she ordinarily behaved. She spoke of family, of church, of God and sin. But having come to America and adopted a new name, she was also trying on a new life, like a department-store sweater, a life in which artists did this, they were destined to come together, to meld, to inspire one another, and then part.

He can't yet bring himself to destroy the painting, to erase

Sarah, Sook-ja from his life, but he knows it is only a matter of time before the painting is found. Still, destruction is so final, and he isn't ready. He shrouds the canvas with a drop-cloth.

As Mr. Zhang is leaving for work, he walks past Calvin's door and hears something inside the apartment that sounds like the flapping of wings. He wonders if the small man is home. That's how he thinks of him, the small man.

And as Mr. Zhang's father is herding the boys, his grandchildren, out of the apartment on their way to school, he sees the building's front door swing shut and the small man in running shorts leap off the stoop.

The run is the same as always. Calvin doesn't vary his route, although he has on occasion reversed the flow, finishing with the Capitol steps instead of beginning there. This morning, though, living deeply inside himself, his mind blank, he lets his feet guide him. He is unaware of his path.

Until, that is, he passes the building where he briefly lived with the other painter and the painter's girlfriend, Cynthia. He realizes now that the woman in the window isn't Sook-ja, or not only Sook-ja. It's partly Cynthia, too. The skin, dark, the face, round—they're both Sook-ja, they're Asian, exotic. But it's Cynthia's hair and, although they aren't visible in the painting, hidden as they are below the window so that only he can see them, in his mind, Cynthia's breasts, her nakedness.

He slows as he passes, gazes up at the loft. Is there movement? It was a game for Sook-ja, a masquerade. Was it the same for Cynthia? Did it mean nothing to her? He speeds on, lets his thoughts ebb, his mind empty.

Jeremy, the painter, was his friend. Or not *his* friend, exactly. A friend of a friend, from the dark days, the hospital. When he came to D.C. from rural Virginia in search of an art scene, a haven, a place to recover, he needed somewhere to crash and Clark, just out of treatment himself, phoned

Jeremy on Calvin's behalf. There was a cot and it wasn't going to be for long. Temporary. Fleeting. He hadn't counted on Cynthia, or on her lovemaking with Jeremy while he lay near them in the dark. He hadn't counted on Cynthia climbing into his cot while Jeremy slept.

When Calvin gets home from the run, sweat-soaked and finally emerging from his depths, like the horizon when dense fog lifts, there's a cop car parked in front of the building. The lights aren't flashing, there's no crowd, the sort that seems to materialize around a crime scene, no agitation of any kind. Inside, there's no sign of the police and, as he enters his own apartment, he wonders if they might not be waiting for him.

But they are not.

As before, he unshrouds the painting and stands naked before it, this time looking for Cynthia in the window, her breasts, her body, visible only to him.

Now it's evening. There is still some stained light in the sky but the apartment is filled with shadows. Calvin sits cross-legged in front of the painting. He lifts a bottle of red wine to his lips—cheap, all they had at the corner store this afternoon, the surly Korean clerk, reminding him of Sook-ja, caged behind hardened glass and bars—and tilts it high because it's nearly empty. He is no longer a drinker, and he knows he will suffer for this. There was a time, though, during a brief stab at college, less a stab than a poke, when it was nothing. It was nothing and everything and it consumed him. It made all the pain worse, it made the scars appear on his wrists, he barely remembers how, although he remembers his knife, and then one day he stopped. One day he stopped and the next day he painted.

There is a soft knock at the door. He's forgotten the painting, which still stands uncovered. He's forgotten, too, that in the past, even before he removed the painting, he rarely came to the door. Not that knocks were frequent. He barely knows his neighbors, in fact knows no one's name and only a few of the faces. But now he stumbles to his feet, the bottle in hand, and he is just about to open the door when he is aware of the face in the window.

"Minute," he says, and sets the bottle on the floor, where it spins and totters before finally tipping noisily. He flings the cloth over the painting, comes back to the door, and opens it.

He doesn't recognize the woman standing before him in her formless shift.

Susanna sees the lack of recognition in his blank face. She is embarrassed, but not surprised. In the time that she and her boyfriend have been living in the front unit, rented from the world-traveling owner, she's rarely seen this small man and spoken to him just once, on a day when she held the door for him as he came in from his run. She asked him something inane then, about the heat or the rain, and he grunted a reply.

"I'm sorry about the painting," she says, pointing behind her toward the blank wall. "I love it. I love standing and looking at it when no one's around. It's like being alone in a museum."

Calvin leans against the door jamb to steady himself.

"The little one of the monument is mine." She lowers her eyes. Her painting is childish, and she knows he knows. "Yours, though. It's perfect."

The air is hot and Calvin feels his throat tighten.

"Anyway. I just wanted to tell you that." She backs away, turns toward her own door. He watches her, the way she moves on tip-toe in her bare feet, how her calves harden with each step, how the hips sway.

"You liked it?"

She stops. She faces him. She nods.

Her face is round and dark, her black hair short. She's

not Asian, she isn't Sook-ja, but she might be Cherokee. It could be her face in the window. The more he looks at her, the brown eyes, the flat nose, the more certain he is.

"Would you like a drink?" He bends to retrieve the empty bottle, and rises, dizzily, waving it in his hand.

She lowers her eyes, nods. Although she doesn't know it yet, only fears it because of her boyfriend's carelessness, she's pregnant. She's not sure what will happen if she is, and so she sees no reason not to go with him. She wasn't lying about the painting. It makes her feel alive, makes her skin tingle, how that silo looks like it might rocket into the sky at any moment. She would go anywhere with this man.

Now there is a second bottle of wine, and glasses. Unsteady, he spills while pouring the girl's glass. This is how he thinks of her, the girl, because he doesn't know her name.

"I don't know your name," he says. He thinks he might have only thought this because the girl says nothing and, in any case, it wasn't a question. He doesn't need to know her name, doesn't want to know her name, can't possibly remember her name. She can be Sook-ja, or Cynthia. It doesn't matter. He gulps his wine.

"Susanna," she says. "You know? Banjo-on-my-knee? Susanna?"

He's staring at her face, picturing it in the barn window, wondering how it is that he's already painted this girl Susanna's face.

"You're Calvin, right? I asked Mr. Artoyen about you." She's looking away again, blushing.

He doesn't know who Mr. Artoyen might be, doesn't recognize the name, although the man is the building's developer and also Calvin's landlord, but he laughs at the sound of his *own* name, at the idea of anyone talking about him when he isn't there. It doesn't seem possible. It implies an existence outside of himself, one that he doesn't control and that therefore has nothing to do with him, and the absurdity of it begins to drag him back into his own cloudy depths.

"What happened to the picture?" She's seen that there is a large canvas covered by a drop-cloth and her eyes flit to it now.

Calvin pours more wine. The air is hot. He gets up and strips off his shirt. She notices his wiry build, his sturdy arms, the film of hair on his chest. He retrieves a sketchpad, sits and begins to work.

"You're drawing me?" She blushes again, tries to hide her face behind the wine glass while, at the same time, watching the image develop on the pad.

It's a furious process, painting. For him it's almost physical, like defecation. And that's what he feels now, for the first time in months, for the first time since Sook-ja. His torso is relaxed, there is a draft that feels cool on his bare chest, he can let go of what's inside, and the work flows. He's holding nothing back.

Susanna doesn't know what to do. Calvin—this is how *she* thinks of him, never "the small man," always "Calvin"—isn't really looking at her anymore. Or, he is: he glances up from the sketchpad now and then, steals a piece of her, that curl of hair that loops under her ear, or the dimple in her chin she's always hated, and then dives again into the sketch to preserve it there, like an insect in amber; but he doesn't *see* her. Should she be still? Should she move closer? Should she unbutton her dress and let it fall? Should she touch him?

She touches him.

And now he looks at her.

Susanna's boyfriend is in his Contracts class at the Georgetown Law Center a few blocks from Nanking Mansion. Time drags; the professor drones. The boyfriend watches a large-breasted blond in the row ahead and imagines sex with her, rehearses the proposition, pictures her reaction, her acquiescence.

It is the blond he will think of when he enters Susanna tonight, and it is the blond he will think of when Susanna tells him about the sketch Calvin has made of her and, almost as an afterthought, that she has let Calvin fuck her.

Aloysius, the neighbor who heard the painting thump against his wall in the night, will hear more thumps, against a different wall, and shouting, unintelligible. A door will slam. There will be a final thump.

Calvin rises early. He stands before his painting of the barn, marvels at the reflection of early light in the whorls of his brush strokes, the barn at dawn, red-tinged. And there is Susanna in the window—Sook-ja, Cynthia—her face calling to him. There is a bed in the studio behind her, hidden from view, but she begs him to come to her. She has promised to visit him again today, to pose for him again, to please him again.

In her own apartment, Susanna is locked in the bathroom, where she has slept curled on the cold tile. She hears her boyfriend's curses, books flung, broken glass. She waits for the front door to open and close so she can go to Calvin. He will protect her. He is her salvation.

It is a crisp morning and Calvin flies toward the Capitol on his run. He comes to the building where Cynthia lives with Jeremy and he gazes up at the window as he passes. He sees her there, thinks he sees her pale face, like the moon, full of longing, and he hardens at the thought of Susanna, who has promised to return. He is aware of the hardness, painful in the tight pouch of his shorts. He is aware of the sweat on his chest, the sweat on his forehead dripping into his eyes. He is aware of traffic, of uneven sidewalks, of gravel and pedestrians. There is a twinge in his right foot, a sharp, distinct jab that he can visualize, one of the tiny bones aggravated by repetition, and he knows that the pain, at this moment a deniable annoyance, will spread.

At this moment, Susanna's apartment door slams shut, followed by a silent vacuum, the deep quiet of absence. She rises from the bathroom floor, gazes in the mirror at her face, at the glowing red welt.

For the first time since he resumed running, Calvin counts the Capitol steps as he jogs up, counts again on the way down. He falls in behind a pair of Marines, the same men he has breezed past on other days. He sees that they are in stride, right, left, right, tiny explosions of dust at each footfall. He hears the flap of their loose t-shirts against their bodies, the faint hum of chatter passing between them as he flags, and they pull away.

The boyfriend waits for the echo of the slamming door to subside. He knows which door belongs to the painter, the bastard who has fucked his Susanna, and his broad, rough hand engulfs the knob. The door is unlocked. He enters. He's seen the little man and he burns to confront him, to warn him to stay away from Susanna, aches to fight him. But the painter is gone. The boyfriend sees the crude barbell, the empty wine bottles, the red crust at the bottom of a lipstick-stained glass. But there is no one to fight, no one on whom to focus his rage, and so the fire dies. He turns to leave. He's preparing to return to Susanna, to apologize, to beg forgiveness if that's what it takes, to seek absolution in her body for the sins of his, when he notices the big painting of the barn, with the face in the window.

The pain in Calvin's foot is almost unbearable now. He hasn't felt pain in so long he barely recognizes the sensation, but it extracts memories he's suppressed, a step-father, young love, the scars on his wrists and the agony of the before and the after, until he found redemption in the brushes and paint. But now the pain brings him to a stop.

Back in Calvin's apartment, the boyfriend is motionless. The face in the window is dark, but clearly it is Susanna. How long have they been hiding their affair? How long has she been cheating on him with this . . . *little man*? He flexes his hands into fists, feels heat rise into his chest, his neck, his face. If the little man were there now he would beat him into sludge. He would beat him until he felt nothing.

Calvin has stopped running. He heads home, limping, feeling, too aware.

The boyfriend looks around the apartment. On a table next to a vacant easel there is a hunting knife, spattered with paint. Like blood, he thinks, the bastard's blood, and he seizes the knife.

It takes hours, seems like hours, for Calvin to get home. He can barely make it up the front steps, struggles with the key, leans heavily into the door to push it open.

Inside his apartment, although he senses something is wrong, he doesn't notice immediately what has happened. But he feels glass underfoot, smells the sweat of an intruder, and then he sees. The easel, its legs and spine broken, lies in a heap, embracing the homemade barbell that has crushed it. Tubes of paint bleed into the wood floor, amidst stained shards of the wine bottles that have been used to flatten them. His back is to the painting, but he already knows. He must turn to see it. He begins to turn and then stops, begins again and then turns just his head, lets the rest follow when his eyes see. The painting—the barn, the phallic silo, the face in the window—is whole. The face mocks him. Blood, or perhaps it is paint, is pooled at his feet.

The old Chinese grandfather, alone in the apartment at the end of the hall, removes the pyramid of oranges from the family altar, dusts the framed photographs of his wife, of his son's wife, and then returns everything to its place. He lights incense, bows, and speaks to the dead.

In the front apartment, Susanna has emerged from the bathroom. The boyfriend is sitting on the floor, his arms and face awash with red. She sits next to him and puts her hands in his.

And Calvin. Now there is no hesitation. He finds the knife, feels its heft, and lunges at the painting of the barn, slicing through the canvas as if it were skin, through the silo, through the angles of the roof, through the half-open door, through the window, the shadowy face in the window.

He steps through the rubble of the studio, pushes aside the shattered easel. He locates an unbroken bottle of wine and uncorks it. He drinks. He feels the pain in his foot abate, feels his mind clear. Blood pulses in his fingers, throbbing through him, engorging him.

He locates the blank canvas that has tormented him and sets it upright against the wall. Brush in hand, he peers into its emptiness. It is like snow, a blizzard that once seemed as though it would last a lifetime but now looks sure to end. Behind the blizzard will be an image that only he can see, that only he can render, his destiny. Perhaps a glittering mountain peak, or the tops of trees. Perhaps a snow-etched roofline. A violin. A banjo. A dark, round face.

LAST LILACS

First Chips went missing, our sweet pug, the black one, the one who licked our faces with his rough little tongue and would wag his whole rear end if we so much as glanced in his direction. And then Sascha, the tan one, who mourned the loss as much as we did, who burrowed under the sofa pillows and glared, two beady eyes peering at us accusingly from his damask cavern. Sascha, who no longer allowed Charles to touch him, would snarl at the sight of him. Sascha, who once loved to romp with Chips and the little demons in the next apartment—those poor boys whose mother died in that horrible accident—and after Chips vanished wouldn't give them the time of day.

It started on a glorious damp Friday, when the daffodils had just opened, bringing color back to D.C. after a bleak winter filled with government scandals and terror alerts. The sunny darlings were everywhere—in the shabby gardens of tenement towers, thriving on otherwise barren roadway medians, even in a tacky vase in the faculty lounge of the blighted school where I taught. As I walked home from the Metro that day, the sight of those buttery trumpets put a spark in my step. I may have whistled—not something I'm known for—and not even the sight of the dreary façade of the Nanking Mansion, where Charles and I had lived since its ill-conceived gentrification, could dim my spirits. Inside, I flung open windows despite the lingering chill, slipped a cheery Stravinsky disc into the CD player, and lit a lilac candle I'd been saving for just this day of awakening. I believe I closed my eyes and let my senses carry me in time, to childhood gardens, to first loves.

And then Charles dragged in, a mess, hair disheveled, coat slathered with mud, and only Sascha was with him, pacing and jumping and nipping at my feet.

"Where's Mr. Chips?" I asked, and I might as well have addressed Sascha because Charles couldn't speak. I turned the Stravinsky down and poured Charles a drink, the citrusy gimlet he favors.

"I took the boys for a walk," he began, after a healthy swallow of vodka. It was their afternoon routine, a treat for all of them to meet and greet at the doggie park. "I suppose I was in a hurry. Distracted."

"Why? What's wrong?"

He flapped his hand at me as though to shoo the question away.

"Anyway, we went the short way, down New York, instead of along M, and it was so ugly I practically had my eyes closed." He closed his eyes as if his disgust needed demonstration.

I could picture the threesome, dodging broken glass and discarded drug paraphernalia, the tiny legs of Chips and Sascha churning like the wheels of wee locomotives to keep up with long-limbed Charles, stopping every so often for him to light a new cigarette or to spoil them with a beefy treat.

"But where's Chips?" I asked.

Charles opened his eyes and downed the rest of his drink.

"As we passed one of those derelict row houses, we were set upon by thugs."

It wasn't funny, of course, but the way he said it nearly brought a smile to my lips that I fought mightily to suppress.

"It happened so fast, I don't know exactly what hit me." In a flash he was sprawled on the sidewalk, his camelhair coat soaking in a puddle, his wallet and bejeweled Cartier chronometer gone, and Chips nowhere to be seen, whether snatched along with everything else or giving heroic chase, Charles could not be sure. Only Sascha was left behind, yapping at the top of his diminutive lungs.

We searched the neighborhood, even as the daylight ebbed. We posted hastily printed fliers with a grainy snapshot. We enlisted the help of our fellow Nanking Mansion residents: the revolting sculptor next door, the insipid hand-holders from the front unit, and anyone else we could conscript, even those awful little boys.

Chips had been a gift, a wedding present of sorts from clients of Charles's, the Van Arsdales, one of those Washington power couples with the glorious Georgetown manse and a fancy horse farm in Middleburg. Charles designed both interiors, from chandeliers to hand towels, powder room to tack room, and the Van Arsdales were so appreciative that they showered him with gifts for years, long after he'd left the business, having grown weary, absolutely nauseous, of the all-time gayest cliché. But when they heard about us, and the elaborate-yet-tasteful ceremony we'd planned to solemnize our commitment to one another and our joint future—not that we could actually marry, of course, not in these Fascist States of America—they showed up in their wedding finery and a picnic basket slung over Mrs. Van Arsdale's arm, looking for all the world like the Tin Man and Dorothy. And, sure enough, out of the basket's checkered-cloth lining popped not Toto but a darling, tiny black pug.

Charles was always a film buff, and I suppose that's where

he found the inspiration for our cutie-pie's name, although as a puppy he did resemble a chunk of very dark chocolate. Whenever Charles left the house in those days—when he didn't take the dog with him, that is—he crooned, "Goodbye, Mr. Chips," and his laughter, his big bellowing, flamboyant laughter, echoed in the Gallery (that horrible lobby of our horrible retro building, where the nasty over-large and indecipherable paintings affront us every time we open our door) and floated after him into the street. We were newlyweds, in a new home, such as it was, and our baby was a constant wonder. It was a delicious time.

Unlike Mr. Chips, Sascha was a rescue situation, and being the product of a dysfunctional home might explain his more distant and suspicious personality, as if he had learned early on in life one of the lessons I'm afraid we all have to face eventually: people can't be trusted. The animal shelter didn't know the poor thing's name, not that it mattered, but when we saw the two pugs together for the first time, checking each other out like a pair of queens in a leather bar, his name just leapt from my mouth, the perfect companion for Chips: "Salsa." Except that Charles, once a student of Russian, heard "Sascha," and that's the name that stuck.

When Charles and I met more than a decade ago through a mutual friend who claimed a talent for matchmaking, I'd recently been dumped by Ned, the love of my life, a pretty, bisexual cellist with the Fairfax Symphony who had decided to focus on the other hemisphere of his appetites and marry the girlfriend I didn't know he had; and Charles, considerably older and already tired of the decorating game, was in mourning for Larry, a watercolorist with whom he'd lived for ages. By the time Chips went missing, we'd been together on and off for ten years, committed for the last three, after we both, independently, arrived at the conclusion that we could do no better.

If Charles was a bored interior designer, I was a decidedly minor poet, so minor that I eked out a living teaching English in a high school where, it cannot be disputed, few of the students could actually read the language, much less wade through verse. If you've come across the saddle-bound literary magazine produced by a certain mid-Atlantic state university with more of a penchant for basketball than poetry, you may have seen my work. But probably not. And, anyway, those were predictable love poems about a certain cruel musician with passionate hands, and they deserve to be ignored.

Although we did have a honeymoon period after the "wedding," it wasn't always champagne and truffles for Charles and me. I suppose I'm as flawed as anyone, but Charles was prone to moody peaks and valleys and, being older, wasn't always responsive when I felt amorous, which left us both frustrated. We'd argue. We'd shout. We'd say things we didn't mean. Charles, on one occasion, even threw an ashtray, a leaded-glass monstrosity that left a crater in the wall that we later hid with a gilt-framed mirror. I didn't think he was aiming at me.

We never cheated on each other, though, even during the rockiest times. That was the whole point of the ceremony, after all, to give ourselves over to the strictures of monogamy, whether sanctioned by church and state or not. I for one was tempted, I admit, or, more precisely, aroused, especially by some of the youngsters in my class, those boy-men with their broad shoulders and simian arms, their youthful, exuberant scent and ever-ready libidos. But, no, that's a path I would not take, could not take. And then there was Ned, my dark, soulful cellist, who came to me in my dreams from time to time. But I knew there was no going back. The clock doesn't turn that way, then or now. Regret is a fool's errand. As for Charles, meaning this with all the love and affection in the world, but recognizing that time and loss have taken their toll, who else except me would have him?

Especially in those days. Although never truly attractive—I'd seen old photographs and it's a product, in my estimation, of the equine nose and the receding chin, features that did not work well together, particularly on a tall man—Charles, when he was in the decorating business, at least wore sharp, designer suits, stylishly loud ties, and shoes that could blind a careless admirer. With no clients to impress once he put the business behind him, his days spent online trying to outwit the stock market, Charles banished the slick wardrobe to the back of the closet. He smoked and drank more, occasionally forgot, or at least neglected, to bathe, and some days didn't bother to dress at all. But after Chips went missing, his slide accelerated. He let his stock portfolio, once a carefully tended garden, go to seed and weed, failing to even touch the computer for days at a stretch and, more often than I wish to admit, not leaving the bed except when nature commanded.

Nagging only made his sullenness more pronounced.

"Talk to me," I'd say.

He'd look at me from the bed, eyes sad as an Emily Dickinson poem, and dismiss me with a feeble wave.

It wasn't what you might think. We were both tested regularly. We both knew plenty who'd gone in the plague—I thought of it more as a tsunami wiping out whole villages of our people—and that was unspeakably tragic, God knew. And of course there was Larry, Charles's partner whom I never met and about whom Charles spoke seldom. But if that were the curse upon him then, I would have known. No, it was something else. As I say, though, it got worse when those beasts snatched poor Mr. Chips, and Charles, my old darling, simply reeked—of life, of cigarettes (the unfiltered sort he insisted upon), of gin—and Sascha, the little snip, was offended.

While our loss dropped Charles into a tailspin, it unleashed in me a creative urge I hadn't felt in years. The day Chips disappeared, in fact, as Charles slept off the gin anesthetic, I put pen to paper and actually wrote coherent lines of poetry: *The portrait shouts to mem'ry's whisper, the album grasps what wisdom cannot hold*... Derivative stuff, I knew, Auden would have been appalled, but the point is the verse flowed. And there was more. I borrowed Whitman's lilacs, a personal favorite, and summoned memories long forgotten. I had so much to say, and for the first time there was nothing to silence me, not my parents, not grief over Ned's perfidy, not Charles's well-intentioned criticism. Nothing. In a matter of days I had a dozen or so poems, my best work, words I thought the world needed to hear, and although my hand trembled as I affixed the stamps to the envelope, I sent them off to that same obscure magazine in whose pages my lyrics had once appeared. They understood me then; surely they would understand me now.

Another incident bears mention, one that Charles didn't even know about. Although he made it out to be something more, I suspected his mugging while walking Chips and Sascha was just that: a mugging, no more, no less. The brutes were after money and maybe they took Chips on a lark, thought he was worth a few dollars on the black doggie market. But not long ago I was walking home from the Metro—as I do each weekday, strolling the few blocks along M Street between the station and our building—and instead of being alert to my surroundings, one of the first rules of urban survival, I was engrossed by the sight of workmen on scaffolding engaged in the much-needed renovation of the Victorian duplex on the corner. I was thus preoccupied when two men stepped out of the shadows into my path.

"May I help you?" I asked, knowing that help was not what these two were after, but possessing a sadly limited arsenal of greetings for threatening strangers. My entire body pulsed with fear.

The men laughed.

It wasn't as if this was a new experience. Gay men get it all the time simply because they're different, even in relatively tolerant Washington. Even in their own families. It's another cliché, only because it's so true, but in my family I was an outcast. My father, a man whose life consisted of drinking too much bourbon and selling automotive fan belts, who reeked of the burned-flesh smell of industrial rubber and whose hands bore permanent black streaks from handling the stuff, must have known, even before I did, that he and I were not much alike. As a boy I assumed we were. He played golf, but no other sports that I was aware of, and I certainly made no pretense of athleticism. He maintained the yard at home and I puttered in my mother's garden—that's where my fondness for flowers was born—thinking that the work was something we shared. In truth, we shared nothing. When, in high school, I began to realize that I was attracted to men, that I stood apart from everyone of my acquaintance, I also came to understand why my father had all those years kept his distance: he was repulsed by what he saw in me. I scarcely needed to say anything to him about my self-discovery, knowing that he already knew, but when I finally did—more because I had questions about my place in the world than anything else, and there was no one else to ask—he said he didn't want to hear about it, that it wasn't something he would discuss. And we never *did* discuss it, that or anything else. My mother, a woman from whom I inherited my love of literature and my disdain for confrontation, followed my father's lead, as she did in all things. Then there was my older brother, who brought home names to call me, collected them like younger kids might hoard marbles or baseball cards, and regularly trotted them out to hurl in my direction.

But these two men accosting me on the street in my own neighborhood were strangers, and the words they used, the names they called me there in public as I tried to pass by them, wounded me in a way my own family could not. These men didn't know me. They didn't have my memories of loving Ned, of being crushed by him. They didn't know how comforted I was to find Charles. They didn't know anything about me. How could they say these things?

So I was no stranger to what Charles had been through: the loss of Chips, the thuggery on the street. But it didn't derail me as it did Charles. I was writing again. I saw poetry in everything, images that stirred my soul. I'd rediscovered flowers. I'd placed vases throughout the condo and filled them with whatever was available at Eastern Market on Capitol Hill, or even the tawdry kiosk in the grocery store. I'd never spent much time in the alley behind our building—it's a trash-filled eyesore—but there was an overgrown lilac bush in a neglected corner, and I was already looking forward to appropriating a few of its blooms. I knew it wouldn't be long.

The ugly pug's absence, then, affected us differently, but we both missed Chips like you'd long for a missing child. And that made it all the more disconcerting on the day that Sascha was nowhere to be found.

After some weeks of enduring his decline, I came down one morning with some idea of what to expect since Charles had not made it to bed the night before, and a pattern had emerged. I'd given up trying to extract some explanation from him. Sure enough, there he was, asleep on the sofa, an ashtray on the floor, filled, overflowing, smoke still fogging the air. An empty booze bottle lay cradled in his arms. Hackneyed, but no surprise.

What *was* a surprise, though, was the open front door. And no sign of Sascha.

I shook Charles. "Sascha's gone," I said. "I'm going to look for him." I ran out without knowing if my words had registered, and spun around in the empty, ghastly hallway, gazing at 12 identical closed doors, as in some surreal nightmare. He wasn't in the Gallery, plainly, and where else could he be?

I headed outside and started east, but then backtracked, turned south, each direction as improbable and futile as the last. It was a big world, with new scents and sights that would entice the most satisfied of animals. And poor Sascha, with Chips gone and moody Charles not to be trusted, maybe he was ready for a change. It hit me as I came back to Nanking Mansion that we'd never see our boy again. On top of that, I'd rushed off without my keys. I knew I'd have to face Charles, that he'd be devastated and unrelentingly morose, but I couldn't just then, not yet, and I sank to the curb and wept.

I'd had it rough, but Charles's life hadn't been a bed of lilacs, either, to torture another trite expression. Among other things, he hadn't known his father long enough to be shunned by him. Charles eventually told me, after we'd been together for years, that his father blew his brains out with a shotgun when Charles was six. I've seen the brittle, yellowed clippings. His mother had concocted a fiction about a fatal automobile accident, and it wasn't until Charles was away in college—by which time the pattern of their two-way lies had become customary—that he learned the truth. When, at Christmas, or Easter, or some other dismal family gathering, Mrs. Simpson pulled a locked jewelry box from the closet, opened it, and handed the faded newsprint to her son, it came as no real surprise to him that everything he'd always been told, every aspect of the picture his mother had painted of his father, turned out to be false. And he retaliated by telling her the truth about himself.

Charles's mother didn't so much shut him out after that as construct a fantasy world, one in which her husband would be home momentarily—from work, the dry cleaners, a business trip—and her son, the architect, doctor, lawyer, was due for a visit, with his beauty-queen, college-professor wife and adorable children. Charles couldn't take it anymore, rarely saw her, and never spoke of her. It didn't seem possible that she was the reason for his funk, no matter what news he'd had of her. If not family, then what?

But Sascha. Where could he be? I finally steeled myself to face Charles and rang our buzzer.

"Did you find him?" he asked when he let me in. "Where is he?"

I couldn't look into Charles's eyes. I shook my head.

"Maybe he's in one of the other units?" If our apartment door had been open, then, too, might someone else's, and Sascha might, unbeknownst to the occupants, have wandered in, hunting for treats or, possibly, Mr. Chips, and so might have been trapped inside when the door closed. "Maybe?"

We knocked on doors.

In Mr. Zhang's apartment, the two little boys, Simon and Wesley, helped us search. They looked everywhere, even insisting that we come into their toy-strewn bedroom just to prove that Sascha wasn't hiding, or being hidden, there. On the way back downstairs I inhaled the smoke of sandalwood incense burning on a table-top shrine, decorated with a pyramid of tangerines and a photograph of Mrs. Zhang. I believed in nothing, but said a little prayer for Sascha. Before we left, Charles spent a few minutes checking the kitchen, suspecting, I suspected, that Mr. Zhang or his old father might have an unquenched taste for dog.

Next we knocked on the door of our newest neighbor, Aloysius, a mysterious young lawyer we rarely saw. To our surprise he was home and opened his apartment to our search; we followed him into the unit, a space even larger than our own.

"Sascha," Charles called melodiously, stopping only

momentarily to observe, I think, that there wasn't a stick of furniture in the place, far beyond modern minimalism. Its unfettered wood floors glimmered, and dust motes danced in sunbeams pouring through un-curtained windows. Our footsteps echoed in the emptiness. Upstairs, a pigeon, having entered, according to our neighbor, through the ragged hole in the brick wall, the provenance of which he didn't explain, wandered haltingly across the expanse. But no Sascha.

We knocked on every door in turn and managed to search just two more apartments, without success.

Back in our own apartment, Charles fixed a drink and, despite the early hour, I joined him. With Chips, I felt, we'd allowed ourselves too long to hope he would be returned to us, and that made the loss when we finally accepted it that much more difficult to absorb. Now I had a different outlook. Loss can be prepared for and managed; loss can motivate, stimulate.

"We have to face the possibility," I said, ever pragmatic, "that our little one is gone for good."

"Don't talk like that," Charles said, but his eyelids drooped, the flesh sagged in his cheeks.

When my family rejected me, I knew instinctively where to find comfort. The garden filled me, and there was solace in Auden, wisdom in Whitman. It seemed unlikely that their images could revive Charles, who'd never been enthralled by poetry, but I wasn't thinking only of him when I went to the bookshelf. These men understood longing and loss. They understood me.

"'Ever-returning Spring, trinity sure to me you bring, Lilac blooming perennial and drooping star in the west, And thought of him I love.'"

Charles covered his face with his hands and sank to the couch as I read the Whitman poem.

"What's wrong?" I asked.

Charles fought for control, opened his mouth to speak, but stopped. He took a deep breath. "Larry," he said.

Charles almost never spoke of Larry. He once told me that he'd loved Larry deeply but that he refused to live in the past. He couldn't love a dead man. He rocked forward and back on the sofa.

"It's been ten years," he said. "I miss him."

"Of course you do," I said. I dropped my hands on his shoulders to slow the rocking. His body still swayed. "That's what's been bothering you, then."

Now he stopped. Another deep breath. "No."

There was a time when we talked. He used to tell me all the indignities he suffered, each perceived slight. He even told me when he nicked himself shaving, as if I couldn't see the blood on his cheek.

"I'm going to see my mother," he said. "I phoned. It had been so long. She didn't know me."

The apartment was silent. I slipped the Whitman back on the shelf, his words lingering in my head like a scent. Why now? After all this time. I sat next to Charles, wrapped an arm around his trembling shoulders.

"For how long?"

"I don't know," he said. "A while."

The lilac bush in the alley was a mystery. It sprawled over a high privacy fence and drooped to the ground heavy with the season's last burst. I didn't ask why this treasure was there, in that forsaken place. I didn't ask whether I deserved this gift. With my shears I snipped an armful of blooms, and let the sweet air envelop me as I carried them inside.

While Charles packed, his decision made, I arranged the lilacs in a vase. I thought of my own mother, her flowers. Charles had made a choice, and I suspected he didn't mean to come back. No matter what it was that troubled him, how could he so casually discard the union we'd worked so hard to build?

I fixed another drink. I sliced a lime that filled the kitchen with its bite. I tasted the cold gin on my tongue, crushing the ice, like daggers against my teeth. He wouldn't come back. He would take care of his mother and she would linger and he would stay. I finished my drink and made another.

The mail came. I opened an envelope I recognized, addressed to me in my own hand. "Dear Writer, we regret that your manuscript does not suit our present needs." I read it twice, tried to recall what I'd written, *the portrait shouts to mem'ry's whisper*, and crumpled the letter in my hand.

There was a knock on the door, barely audible. I shoved the letter into my pocket, and the knock came again, louder. As downtrodden as I have ever felt in my life, I pulled the door open.

Sascha! There he was, squirming in the arms of our Chinese neighbor, his boys at his sides. Behind them stood a dark, slender man, eyebrows arched, a nervous grin. Ned.

It seemed impossible that Ned should appear, just when the memory of him had been haunting me. The last time I'd seen him, and the time before that and several before that, it had been from afar. His orchestra had grown in fame and he had grown with it. I sat where I hoped he would not see me and watched his flowing hair dance as he played, watched him inhabit the music as he'd once inhabited our life together.

"We search," said Mr. Zhang. "Up and down street."

My eyes were on Ned.

"He found a friend," said the older boy. "Another dog. A big dog."

Sascha practically leapt into my arms, licking and wriggling, while I couldn't look away from Ned, certain that if I did he would vanish, and then Charles was there reaching for Sascha, cooing and clucking between heaving sobs. He, too, stared at Ned. Why was Ned here?

"Thank you," I said to Mr. Zhang, shaking his hand and then the hands of the boys. "Thank you." I reached for my wallet, but Mr. Zhang shook his head. "Thank you," I said again.

Then they were gone, and Ned stood alone in the doorway. Over the years, he'd changed little. He still let a black curl dangle over his forehead, still wore crisp, black slacks and a white shirt, as if he could grab his cello and appear in a concert at a moment's notice.

"You didn't return my calls," he said.

I backed away from the door, wondering if I'd heard him correctly. Ned had called? Charles moved deeper into the living room and set Sascha on the floor, then sank into the couch. Sascha jumped to his side and danced on the cushion, his old aloofness vanished. Then he was off again, sniffing, exploring. Looking for Chips. Charles sat with his back to me, gazed toward the wall.

"I left messages," Ned said. "I spoke with Charles."

Mem'ry's whisper, I thought. He called and he'd spoken with Charles. My eyes went to the phone—a wireless contraption we kept on a sideboard near the bottom of the stairs along with a vase, now filled with the lilacs I'd cut—as if I might see there the messages Ned had left, some explanation for what had happened to them. But none was needed.

I looked from Charles to Ned and back. I tried to swallow, but my throat was constricted and dry. The scent of lilacs came to me.

"I shouldn't have come," Ned said. And as suddenly as he had appeared, he was gone, like a passing cloud. I didn't run after him. I realized when I heard the door close that I hadn't said a word.

I woke in the dark, hours before dawn, alone in our bed, aware that this was how it would be from now on. I heard something, unfamiliar, but familiar, and of course I knew it was Charles, not yet departed. I stroked the sheet, felt his cool absence. I listened. The sky rumbled, a window rattled. It had never been so dark, not ever, and I fumbled for my slippers at bedside. I inched my way to the stairs and down, stopping midway. A whimper floated up, meeting distant thunder. Down the rest of the way, blind. I turned at the bottom of the stairs and collided with the vase I'd put there, the flowers, the lilacs I could smell but not see. I flailed, my fingers grazing blooms as the arrangement fell, the glass shattering noisily, water rushing at my feet.

"Charles?" I took a step, felt glass beneath my slipper. I took another step and inhaled the fragrance of crushed lilac. "Charles?"

"I think he wanted to go."

My eyes began to adjust. I could make out the dim silhouette of Charles on the sofa, head in his hands. A bottle on the table, a cigarette burning. The door was open.

"Who, Charles?"

"I know he did. He begged. What else could I do?"

Two suitcases stood by the door.

"You don't have to go right now, do you?" I took another step, more glass, and this time I felt it pierce the slipper and my sole. I couldn't move.

"I kept his number. It's there. By the phone." Charles finally looked at me and in the spreading light I could see his pleading eyes, the memory of a lifetime.

I pictured poor Sascha, still mourning Chips, scratching at the door. Desperate to search, to reclaim what he'd lost. Hungry for belonging, a desperate need to connect. And there was Charles, the solution, the key to the wide world.

THE GAME OF LOVE

Susanna shoves Thomas away. She hates this. She pleads with him, silently, to stop. A scowl shades his thin face.

"Bitch," he says, almost spitting the word. He approaches again and she thrusts her hands at his chest, sending him sprawling onto their bed. He's tall and lean, all arms and legs that flop comically as he falls.

He rises, seizes her wrist. She yanks free.

He comes at her and she slaps his cheek; his pale face blooms red. He's breathing hard now. She smells the beer on his breath. He comes again.

"Harder," he pleads.

She swings hard, her palm open; the smack against his jaw stings her hand.

"Now me," she says and lunges at him.

He grabs her shoulders and manages a feeble slap. She knows that's all he's willing to give, that he doesn't believe she wants more, because in truth she doesn't. She's tried to tell him how much she hates it, and sometimes he remembers. But never mind. The game has had its desired effect. It's over, for now.

He comes toward her again and now her touch is light. Her hands linger on his chest, half push, half caress. She walks him back to the bed, pulls his damp t-shirt over his head, and he falls back, taking her with him. Nothing matters now but being with him, feeling him, all of him, tasting him, taking him into her mouth if that's what he wants, taking him inside her, devouring him, being devoured.

Now he's on top and their clothes tear away: her t-shirt and shorts, his jeans. There is no time for protection. The need is too urgent. He's in, and racing. She feels him slowing, trying to prolong for her sake, but she begs him to go faster, harder, because of what it does for him, how it spurs him, how it enlarges him. She screams for it, and now there is no slowing, no stopping until he is empty and she is full.

She lives for these times, after the game she despises, when he is more than her best friend, when she can coax this fire from his body.

Afterward, in the dim light—as they let the game recede and return to themselves, as he breathes steadily beside her—she watches his hairless chest rise and fall, and she thinks about what they'd failed to do, the precaution they had not taken. She knows it's impossible, but she feels the new life beginning, a boy, she's sure of it, and as a child yet herself she wonders what mysteries await him.

In high school, not so long ago, they'd been inseparable. Thomas and Susanna, tall and short, light and dark, always together. His father taught literature at the women's college in their town, a dying red-brick institution on a hill overlooking the withering shops of Main Street. Her father had disappeared when she was a baby, so long ago that she claims not to remember him, although there is a fragrance, a particular brand of minty soap, that triggers a blurred image she thinks is him. His mother had stayed home with the kids, Thomas and his sister. *Her* mother, left with nothing when Susanna's father fled, was a nurse, never failing her only child, providing everything Susanna could want, except a father.

Thomas had known from their first kiss, he has told her repeatedly, that they would be together forever. He could see it in her shining dark eyes, he says, how she looked at him, how her lips didn't want to leave his. She tries to remember, whenever he tells the story, tries to feel the same. She *does* remember the first time they made love, how there'd been anger beforehand over something petty, his habitual lateness maybe or her insecurity, her jealousy. He'd become forceful, taking control, moving beyond their longstanding friendship. And so the game had begun.

They're going to be married. There's been no proposal, no ring, but it's assumed, by his family, her mother, her.

After high school, they'd both enrolled at the local community college so they wouldn't be separated. She didn't finish—there was no money, and, she admitted to her mother, she didn't mind. Her classes had held no interest for her and she didn't keep up. She and Thomas would be together and eventually there'd be a family to raise, and there seemed no point to it. Thomas then entered the university in the next county, and when he was accepted to law school in D.C. it was understood that she would come with him. Marriage would follow, the families assured themselves; the arrangement would be brief. But in the meantime, Susanna would work while Thomas went to classes, and they built the foundation for their lives together. Susanna doesn't remember a discussion about this plan. It had been a given.

And now here they are, with a sweet deal on rent—the owner of the condo, a novelist who's living in Paris, or Berlin, Susanna isn't sure which, is a friend of Thomas's father—and they're finding their way. She's added what she considers homey touches: hand-me-down towels and sheets; miscellaneous plates and pots; posters from their respective childhood bedrooms (Garth Brooks for her, Faith Hill for him); three stuffed animals (her favorites, out of a collection of dozens), including a possibly valuable antique teddy bear; the easel and paints she had started to experiment with during Thomas's demanding senior year of college.

When they had first arrived in D.C., before his law classes started, they'd spent every moment together. Partly it was out of fear. Having moved from a rural, largely homogeneous community, their diverse neighborhood wasn't what they were accustomed to. Each story Susanna heard about a robbery or a mugging—one of the residents of their building had been attacked in broad daylight just down the street, his watch ripped from his wrist—sent a new wave of panic through her. And so they had clung to each other, holding hands, arms entwined, as if each drew energy from the other and would run down and collapse if unplugged.

Even after Susanna had taken a job at the coffee shop on Seventh Street, in the shadow of the gaudy Chinatown arch, and Thomas had immersed himself in his studies, they spent as much time together as they could. There were few friends or distractions. Their only shopping, since money was perpetually tight, was for groceries, and they did that as a team, scouring the Safeway on O Street for bargains, strolling hand-in-hand through the canned-goods aisle, shoulder-to-shoulder in produce. When they'd run through their savings and found that her coffee shop wages didn't go far, Thomas asked his father for help. Vowing never to bear that humiliation again, Thomas found a job waiting tables at a restaurant after classes. But that meant they were apart at night as well as during the day. Susanna couldn't stand being alone—the whole point of her coming to D.C. was to be with him—so for a while she had joined him at work and the owner let her sit at a rear booth. That came to an end when Thomas saw the man's hand on Susanna's shoulder, creeping down her back.

So now each night she waits in the apartment for him to come home, no less afraid than on their first night in the city. On *this* night, to distract herself, she paints, working from a magazine photograph of the Washington Monument surrounded by American flags. From the overhead light fixture there is glare on the glossy page that dilutes her concentration, sparks fantasy. She imagines her painting among others that hang in the building's shared hallway, The Gallery, where the true artists among her neighbors display their collages and massive oils. She imagines, too, that her pathetic painting might be her future, that the road she's on—following after Thomas, living his life story—might not be the only road for her. And she sees, when she lets her imagination take her that far, an exit: Thomas with a leggy, blond waitress, Thomas with a busty classmate, Thomas with any other woman, playing his game.

She hears his key in the lock, puts down the brush, and meets him at the door. She wraps her arms around him, presses her face into his chest, inhales his warm, sour scent, feels his lips press against her hair, and then she releases him. She hasn't seen him since dawn and she watches him now as he takes a beer from the refrigerator and pops it open, swallows the surging foam. He empties his pockets on the counter: a ring of jangling keys; change that clatters free, a quarter that rolls and drops to the floor, where it spins and finally falls; a wad of bills. He smoothes the bills into stacks, counts them—one hundred and fifty seven dollars, he tells her, a decent night, not great—and makes a single pile. He opens a cabinet, the one farthest from the refrigerator, and pulls out a mug, part of the mismatched set Susanna brought from home, and retrieves a roll of bills held together by a rubber band. He adds the new cash and returns the money to its hiding place.

He drinks the rest of his beer while they recapitulate their unexceptional days: one of the girls at Susanna's coffee shop scalded her hand on the milk steamer; a guy in Thomas's study group dropped out of sight. She decides not to tell him about the baby, not yet. She's sure, but it's too soon. He glances at her painting without comment. He comes to her, taps her cheek with his open palm, a grin on his face.

"Bitch," he says.

She finishes her painting of the Monument. She doesn't care that it's amateurish, that the proportions are all wrong and there is no depth, as if the great tower and its flags exist on a single flat plane, united forever in one dimension. They're like her: shapeless and without life.

There is a spot on the wall in The Gallery where the picture would fit and she hangs it there. She stands back to admire her work, but is drawn instead to the large canvas next to it, a colorful abstract in which she thinks she sees a window and a face. This is real art, a gift of imagination, the product of love for the woman in the window. She wonders about the woman, dark like herself. Is she a prisoner behind that window?

At the coffee shop she takes orders, makes the fancy coffee drinks, and studies her customers. The women, she dreams, might be suitable for Thomas. They're young professionals, accountants and lawyers. He's skyrocketing toward a career and they might fit. Not like her. They have style and education. They enjoy the game.

She recognizes one of her customers, Mr. Zhang, the Chinese man from their building, the one with the two little boys and no wife. He sits at a table with an Asian woman Susanna has also seen in the building. She makes a point of passing nearby. She wants to be noticed, to be remembered as a neighbor. She wants to connect. She wipes nearby tables with a damp cloth and bends to pick up imaginary trash at their feet, but Mr. Zhang and the woman speak only to each other. Even amidst the smell of coffee in the shop, like old cigars, so strong it sometimes turns her stomach, Susanna detects a scent of mint, although from the man or the woman she can't tell.

On the way home from work she thinks about the Chinese man and his boys, what it would be like to take care of them, to be loved and needed by them. And she thinks about Thomas and the classmate she has imagined for him, the waitress she's concocted, and they seem so real to her that she is convinced, if something were to happen to her, to their bond, Thomas would not be alone. That perhaps, even now, Thomas is not alone.

On a night when Thomas is especially late getting home, when she would ordinarily be asleep, she waits up for him. She pictures the classmate, the waitress. She remembers blond hairs found on Thomas's jacket, his declining enthusiasm for the game. Or thinks she remembers. It all means something. It's evidence. Their end will come, time will expire, and what will she do then? The baby, if there is a baby—what will become of him?

She sips weak tea, occasionally glances at a *People* magazine she brought home from the shop, featuring an epidemic of celebrity pregnancies, and she waits. It's time to confront him. She rehearses what she'll say.

He comes in finally, quietly.

"You're up late," he says in a midnight whisper. He doesn't come close, he doesn't bend down to kiss her.

"You're *home* late," she says.

"Carmine—I told you about him, right, the new guy?—Carmine and I grabbed a beer after closing." Thomas empties his pockets, counts the bills and adds them to the mug.

"No," she says. "I don't think you mentioned him. Is he the one with long blond hair?" She sounds shrewish, her voice high and sharp. She can't help it. It's happening so fast, like a carnival ride spinning out of control. She once thought they'd be together forever, that his road was hers. She thought it because everyone said so, but what if everyone was wrong? What if *she* was wrong?

"What? No. What are you talking about?"

"Don't lie to me, Tommy." Now her voice is louder than she intends. She feels herself growing angry, just like she feels the life growing inside her, and she doesn't want to be angry. This isn't the game anymore. The game is over.

"I told you. Carmine and I—"

"Stop!" She jumps from the chair, spilling cold tea onto the magazine, and faces him. At the sight of his eyes, his guileless, unrepentant eyes, she lunges. Despite the baby, the protectiveness she feels for him, she pounds Thomas's chest with her fists, slaps him, first with her right hand, then with her left. He steps back, raises his hands to ward off her blows, but it doesn't stop her.

"Take it easy, Sooz," he says, and that drives her to attack harder, faster. She lands blows to his ear, his stomach. She kicks, she knees, she pushes him against the wall. He's cornered, and as soon as the back of his hand connects with her cheek, as the slap, like a gunshot, still resounds in their narrow kitchen, he reaches for her.

"God, I'm sorry," he says.

She shoves him away.

He approaches and she slaps him hard. He staggers back, eyes wide.

She runs to the bathroom and locks the door.

The large painting she admires in The Gallery disappears. Where it had hung there is now only an expanse of white outlined with grime. She closes her eyes and sees the picture, the bright, deep sky, the brown angles that knifed through it, the thick soaring silo that makes her think of the artist, surely a man. There is a painter in the building, a small, red-haired man she has seen running, his pale, sinewy legs churning along the street, his t-shirt soaked with sweat on his return. She guesses that the painting is his work and so she knocks on his door. She misses the painting and wants to tell him.

He answers; she enters and is mesmerized by him, by the smell of paint in the apartment, oily and sweet, by the painter's own loamy odor, by his grey, bird-like eyes. He offers wine and she drinks, although she knows, if she truly is pregnant, she shouldn't. He finds his pad and sketches her; she lowers her eyes, afraid to look at him, to find out that this is his game, like Thomas's game. But she does look, and perhaps it is a game to him, but she doesn't care. There is tenderness in the drawing. Her clothes come off, and so do his.

Another day she visits the sculptor. He moves in a cloud of smoke when he shows his work. He asks her to model for him. Is it the child that makes her behave this way? Her clothes come off, and his.

Susanna lies in bed, waiting, listening. Music plays in the distance, loud enough to hear, too soft to recognize: a radio in the sculptor's studio, or the gospel choir from the church on the corner. Thomas's key turns in the lock, light flows under the bedroom door, the refrigerator opens and shut. A beer can fizzes. Coins rattle on the counter. Dishware clinks. And then cabinets open and bang closed, drawers, the fridge again, the stove, muttered curses, cabinets again, drawers. She closes her eyes, feigns sleep, clutches the blanket and braces.

"It's gone," Thomas shouts. He bursts into the bedroom and turns on the lights.

She looks up at him from the bed, blinking at the ceiling fixture. She clutches her ancient teddy bear. "What's gone?"

"Did you forget to lock up when you went to work? Someone stole the money." His voice is loud, fast, frantic.

She had thought she might tell him the truth, even though it would send him into a genuine rage, but now that he's convinced himself the money has been stolen maybe she won't have to. She'll wait, see what happens. The night she spent in the bathroom, before he begged forgiveness, before he promised that it was some craziness that had come over him, as the slap looped over and over again in her mind, the crack of his hand against her face reverberating, she had developed the plan: take the money, the nest egg her mother never had, accuse him of blowing it on coke, a brief habit from college that maybe he hadn't given up, or the girlfriends she'd invented for him, or a new vice, gambling or prostitutes. But let him think it was stolen. The neighborhood is still iffy. There've been thefts. The painting in the hallway disappeared, after all. It could happen. She would confess to leaving the door unlocked. It was her fault. She'd admit it, say she was sorry, beg forgiveness. One thousand two hundred and eleven dollars. Safe. In case she needs it. But she'll tell him she's sorry about the door. He'll forgive her.

She slips on a t-shirt and follows him back to the kitchen. He opens the cabinet and shows her the empty cup. As she watches he searches again. All the cabinets, the drawers.

"How could you be so stupid?" It isn't a question. It's an angry accusation. The veins on his neck throb as he begins the search anew. "Stupid bitch," he says, eyes wet with rage, no play in his voice. "Cunt." The word is deep in his throat, a growl.

She leans against the fridge, arms crossed over her stomach. Thomas's beer sits on the counter. She reaches for it, lifts the can and drinks, lets the bitterness fill her. The plan shifts once more.

"You can tell me the truth," she says. "I won't be mad."

He has taken all their motley collection of cups out of the cabinet. He looks inside each one, runs his hand over the dark, vacant shelves. He stops and gapes at her, a cup in hand.

"I'm sure you had your reasons," she says. Her tone is steady, full of understanding.

"What?"

"You took it, didn't you? This search of yours—it's for my benefit. You're doing drugs again. Or you took it for your new girlfriend." She has almost convinced herself.

He hurls the cup at the wall, where it explodes and shoots fragments at their feet. "Jesus, Sooz. You're nuts. You know that isn't true. That stuff's in the past. College. And there's only you. You know that."

"Do I?"

He comes to her, reaches for her. She slaps him, hard. He steps back.

The game is in the past. Throwing isn't part of the game.

When the anger subsides, to deflect him, she tells him about the painting, the one that's missing, how for her it's about goals and achievement, about rising up, breaking out, and how that's missing from her life and always has been but she's only just now made this discovery. She realizes that he's not listening, that he's consumed by the stolen cash and her accusations, and beyond the first mention of the painting he hears nothing. So once again she doesn't tell him about the baby she thinks they've made. She doesn't tell him that she slept with the painter. She doesn't tell him any of it.

"I didn't take the money," Thomas says, "so you must have." He laughs, as if the notion is absurd, or as if he wants her to think he thinks it's absurd. Still, he resumes the search.

He flips through the books on the shelf in the bedroom: his heavy, brown law texts, her flimsy romances. He opens their dresser and empties the contents onto the floor. He pulls all their clothes off the hangers in the closet. He checks inside every shoe. She sits on the edge of the bed, watching him. She thinks of anything except the hiding place: the painting, the painter; how she trembled when he sketched her; how he was gentle at first when he took her in his arms; how his taut body, with its paint-spatter constellations of freckles, covered her like a blanket, how she felt it when he came, how she wanted more, wanted him to protect her and her baby. Thomas ransacks the medicine cabinet, strips the bed, tosses her stuffed animals on the mound of clothes and sheets and blankets, and she expects to see the pyre burst into flames, a fitting end to her world.

And because it's the end, because there's no reason not to, she tells him what she's been remembering: the painter's pale thighs joining hers, the wetness inside her, the press of his fine, fiery hair against her own.

Thomas flies from the apartment. She knows he is going to the painter's and she doesn't know what to do. She wants to protect the painter, but she wants to protect Thomas, too. And the baby. And so she remakes the bed, hangs the clothes in the closet, arranges the shoes. She hears shouting, through walls, across The Gallery; she hears breaking glass, the shriek of shattered wood. Quiet descends, like a lull in the storm, and she waits for it to begin again. Thomas doesn't return.

In the morning, when Thomas still has not appeared, she prepares for work. She places the stuffed animals on the bed, resting on the pillows as always. Except for the bear. She turns the bear over, pulls on a loose stitch and opens the bear's back. She moves the wad of bills to her purse.

The next day, at the usual time, perhaps a bit earlier, Thomas comes home. Susanna has restored the cups and glasses to their cabinets. She's swept the shards of the mug from the floor, from under the refrigerator. The money is now hidden behind her painting that hangs in The Gallery, the one Thomas didn't notice. She's confident that no one will disturb her worthless painting, that the money is safe. Thomas opens a beer and sits at the table. She joins him there but they do not speak. He reaches for her hand, which she lets him take. He leads her to the bedroom, where she lets him pull her t-shirt over her shoulders.

Susanna holds her hand to her belly and feels the baby move; he's restless, like her. She touches her brush to the panel on her easel, adds depth to the vase, shadow to the stuffed bear, highlights to the green apple that sits between them. The painter has been teaching her about shadow, about line and perspective, illusion. On her own, and from the baby, she's learned that it's not just distance that affects how we see the world.

After she'd let Thomas fuck her for the last time, without passion, the game over, when he'd confessed to sleeping with a girl from his class the night he didn't come home, when he begged forgiveness, begged her to marry him, promised they would move away, that he would quit school if that's what she wanted, that they could go back to how things were, she made her choice. She kissed him, the friend she'd known since childhood, her playmate, and slept in his arms.

In the morning, while he was at school, she retrieved the money from the painting in the hall. She called a locksmith. She packed Thomas's clothes and shoes and books in boxes, without lingering over his scent, without examination or hesitation, and piled them on the front stoop. By afternoon the boxes had been rifled by neighborhood kids, Thomas's sweaters liberated, his shoes redistributed, and when he came home from work that night she listened to him howl as he realized what she'd done. He pounded on the door, screamed, threatened. The police were called. Not by her, but by Aloysius, the nice lawyer in the back unit who had promised to help.

And now her cat, the cat she's not supposed to have in this apartment and about which only the Zhang boys know, leaps to the table to study the still life: the vase and the bear and the apple. Susanna goes to the window to see if Thomas is still parked out front. It's been almost four months and most days he comes, if only for an hour, and sits in his car, watching. She considers going outside to speak to him, so he can see for himself what he's done, how the world has changed, but also to tell him about Aloysius, the quiet man they'd never talked to who turned out to be so friendly. She wants to tell him about the cat, Tigger, and her paintings, and about the nice little Zhang boys, and the crazy woman across the hall who lost her job, and she wants to tell him all this because he's her friend, and they've been friends forever.

But Thomas sits there in his car, staring at the building, at her window, and she knows he is blind to the woman she has always wanted to be.

COUNTERPOINT

It's my life, I tell him, and I fuck whoever I want. He comes with his demands: he wants this, she needs that. Who does he think he is? I made him! Created him from nothing, from blood, from heat. It was fucking that made him. Who the fuck does he think he is?

I molded him like a piece of clay, gave him shape, carved his nose to mirror mine. His eyes—black like mine. The dark skin, wild hair the color of charred earth, even the crooked smile—all from me. All of that is mine. His bearing, his height, his ranginess. His fucking arrogance.

He calls and shouts into the phone and I hang up. He comes here, descends like a plague. He pounds on my door. Bastard, he screams, kicking the door. It's nothing to you, why won't you do anything, you heartless bastard!

The hideous mutt of the faggots next door yaps in a frenzy; there is shouting from above, this neighbor, that. Bastard, he yells, and pounds and kicks, and finally I open the door to the mirror.

He sees it, too, and is stunned into silence. Only the fucking dog does not shut up.

He's not a boy. Somehow I thought he was a boy.

His mother was a model. Not a beauty, but a plain girl who would pose for me. I loved her imperfections: the delicate skin, almost blue; contorted teeth she hid behind tight lips; tiny breasts, like smooth stones. In clay she was exquisite. In bed she was voracious. It was long ago. I was young, struggling like everyone else to make my way in a world that I mistrusted.

You cheated on her, he shouts. So much shouting; this he got from her. Of course there were others. How could there not be others? But there was no cheating. When there are no promises, no bond is broken. We fucked. There was a child. He is perhaps not the only one. It is creation. Does he not understand?

He arcs through the studio, wary, unwilling to turn his back now that he has seen me. And I. I cannot take my eyes from him. Self portrait.

But you loved her? No longer shouting, an angry whisper I barely hear.

Love? Has he not seen the work? I ask him. Have you seen it? I speak softly, soothingly; calm begets calm.

Pictures. Disgusting. My mother. To look at her like that.

She came every day until it was finished. Not here. Another time and place. My finest piece. She came at dawn, for the light, and I sketched. The light passed over her face as we worked, filled her, changed her, swirled with the smoke from my lips, between her legs, entering her and it became her. It was the light. And when the light was gone, every day, we fucked. Love? Has he not seen the work?

I came to destroy it.

It isn't here, I say.

There were photographs, and casts, but the original is here. I could never part with it. She is safe, where he will not see. It troubles me not at all to lie to him.

She's dying, he says. Now the anger has vanished from his voice. It is drained, like a body without blood. Despair. I hear despair.

I'm sorry, I say, and I suppose I mean it. She deserves happiness, as we all do. She was exquisite, so real, open. Perhaps she is still.

No. No more of your bullshit.

I mean it, I say. I believe I do, even if my hesitation says otherwise. She came to me as Jane or Janet. I called her Natasha, a name to break with her primitive past. Natasha, she said when I christened her, and I was Boris. We lay in bed, two villains, the sweat of our exertions painting us in late afternoon light. I poured wine on her breasts, tasted the salt and the sweet and named her Natasha. Natasha, she said.

Then help her, he says.

What can I do? Am I a physician? A magician? I see now that the boy is beautiful, more than his mother, more than I. My youth restored. His limbs are strong, shoulders broad. His eyes are limpid, skin clear and smooth, like fresh paint, like moist clay. My hands begin to rise, as if to feel the clay between my fingers.

What is your name?

He gapes. He is hurt that I do not know his name, but how should I know his name when I barely know that he is alive. She told me—I think she told me—when the problem arose. There was a little money then, or not, and I told her to fix it, or not, I didn't care. It was perhaps a lie but I had to make it true; a child was impossible. And then she was gone and forgotten, until now. He calls to tell me he exists and then he is at my door shouting and now he is here standing before me, beautiful and sullen.

Daniel, he says, and now it is my turn to gape.

Daniel, I say. She has given him my true name, to go with the face I have given him. I light another cigarette and the smoke wraps around us both.

Daniel, then. What is it you think I can do for your mother?

The boy is in control of himself now; the fever has passed and behind his eyes he weighs, measures.

There is no money. She wouldn't ask for anything, not from you, not her family. There is only me and there is no money.

Are there not doctors who treat the poor? But this I do not say. Even then she was proud, free, indomitable, giving herself only willingly, and there was no family, no more family, to stop her.

I say, The government will pay, will they not?

I told you, he says, and the anger has returned to his voice. She won't see them. Doctors. No one.

I smoke, there are clouds of it. I pace.

Then money won't help, will it, Daniel?

You heartless, fucking bastard, he shouts. He grabs a knife from my easel, the knife I use for the fine detail in clay, blemishes, wrinkles and lines, and he throws it. Not at me, although perhaps he has considered this, but at the far wall, where it sticks, quivering from its flight and collision, until it surrenders its grip and falls noisily to the floor. Daniel runs to the door. There is melodrama in him; it is an act that almost causes me to smile. He mutters, Bastard, and flings the door open so that it bangs against the baseboard. He hesitates. He wants to slam the door shut, to milk the moment, to make a point. I can see this in his puzzling face: should he reach for the knob, yank it toward him? But the door has swung too far, the timing is wrong, his stance is awkward, and instead of consummating his elegant gesture he resumes his angry run through the hall and out into the street.

I am amused by the visit from my son, this boy-man, defender of his mother. I am amused, but I have lost time. I must work, I must follow my routine, and he has spoiled it.

I cannot work. I stare at the clay and I smoke. I think of Daniel, his angry eyes and quivering chin. My chin. There was a time when I wondered what it would be like to have a son, perhaps a passionate son such as Daniel. I know I could not tolerate a simpering infant or an adolescent. But a young man—with such a son, a companion, I could know love, I think, love that isn't possible between a man and a woman. But Natasha has deprived me of Daniel. She has stolen him, poisoned him against me.

There is a quiet knock on the door and I know that Daniel has returned. I welcome what is possible, that we might come to know one another, despite his grief, despite his antipathy, but in the days since his first visit I have given much thought to Natasha's treachery. It comes and goes, but now that he has returned I feel the fury rise in my throat like vomit.

Come, I say, already too angry to touch the door.

He enters. He is not what I remember. He seems smaller, less important. Less like me. His hair is combed, its wildness tamed. His eyes, too, are flaccid.

She didn't know, he says.

Ah. It was your own idea, then.

Yes.

And when you told her? What did she say?

Nothing. She said nothing.

Although he is most of a man, he is too young for drink. And yet I pour for us both. My son and me. But he will not drink.

Daniel doesn't return. I have said he is welcome, although I'm not sure that I mean it. I'm not sure I can absorb him into my life. There are two Daniels. If he expects more, he does not say. If I expect more, I do not say.

Most of me has forgotten Daniel. I work, because I must. The clay calls to me and demands to be shaped, to be transformed into its true self. Is that not art? The revealing of truth?

I work and I am lost in it. All I can see is what the clay will become, is becoming, is. And as I begin, I see a face in the clay, eyes and teeth, I see limbs and guts and flesh. And that is all I can see.

Time passes. The clay is damp and cool between my fingers, the stuff of life. As I work, the clay exudes the smell of the earth from whence it came, the fragrance of the bloody river that washed it red, the stench of decay that made it rich. The rotting leaves, dead flesh. It covers my hands and arms, fills my nostrils.

Hello. A voice invades the life I am creating with my hands, and briefly I believe it is the clay that speaks. If the clay could speak, its voice would be deep and fluid. I watch, listening with my eyes.

Hello. The voice is pitched high, behind me.

I turn and there is a boy. He isn't the man-boy, Daniel, but a much younger child. For a moment and then another moment I suspect that this is a second son, that Daniel has a brother, or half-brother, that they have all chosen to descend upon me at the same time, but the smoke clears and I recognize the child as the son of my Chinese neighbor, one of the unbearable creatures who romp in the hallway, who throw balls and shriek. He sits on the floor, barefoot, in short pants, my knife in his hands.

Go home, I say.

He studies the knife, the heft of it, the glint of its blade.

I take it from him, perhaps too roughly, and the boy's face melts into tears.

Go home.

I unlock the closet, lift the shroud, and there she stands: Natasha, her naked breast heaving but still, her voice silently calling.

The work resumes. I will not be disrupted. I will not be distracted. The shape of the clay emerges between my hands and I recognize the face, the sharp nose, the pellucid eyes. It's a face I want to see but cannot, as if this half-image, this half-life, is all the clay has to offer, and it pains me. This life I cannot have. I destroy it, as Daniel would have destroyed the image of his mother that so disgusts him. I gouge with my fingers, with the knife, with a mallet and chisel, until the block of clay, the unborn face, is dead.

Another neighbor catches my eye, the girl who lives in the front apartment with her brooding boyfriend. When I see her in the hallway I stare and she feels me staring, for she turns and our eyes meet. I invite her into my studio and she tries to tell me her name but I press my finger to her lips and tell her that our names do not matter, that I'll call her Maggie. Maggie, I say, is a woman with no cares, who loves adventure, who fills the gaps in her life with whatever joy she can seize. Maggie is enchanted and she steps inside my apartment, inside the woman I have created.

She is cautious, at first, and I sense that she has been hurt. There are no bruises, but there is an air. Fear. I reach for her hand and she steps away.

I mean you no harm, Maggie, I say, and it's as simple as that. Her brow smoothes, the arch of her back softens. The tension in her body is gone. She now glides through the apartment, studies this sketch, that painting, a study in charcoal, a pencil rendering of Natasha. This one apparently speaks to her and she stops, reaching her hand toward it, a hand that I take. She doesn't flinch.

Do you like that one?

She's beautiful.

Yes, I say. Like you.

Maggie's face burns red, as red as if I've struck her. I am charmed with this Maggie. I lead her to the modeling platform where a stool waits as if for her, bathed in light. And so it begins. She sits and I sketch. She unbuttons the blouse, she reveals a shoulder, she removes the blouse. You will live always in clay, I tell her, and she laughs, a nervous, shrill laugh, and I see she is not sure what I mean.

In bed she is the Maggie I imagine, adventurous, willing, hungry, filling the holes of her life.

From a sketch of Maggie, I work now in clay. She has come several days in succession. We work when the light is good and then we fuck. She says her boyfriend is away, as if she should explain, but I wave my arm and dismiss the boyfriend, wherever he is. We fuck and work.

And now I will bring her to life.

I am working alone when there is a knock on the door. The knock brings a smile to my face because I know it is Daniel, come back to me. What I have envisioned can still be.

But it is not Daniel. It is Natasha. She is gaunt and pale standing in my door, with the dim light of winter showing gray against her skin. There is a scarf, no hair peeking out. She clutches a strip of paper on which numbers and words are written in smudged strokes. There is more life now in the sculpture than there is in the woman. She is small, reduced.

And yet she is the mother of my son. I stand aside and let her in. She shows no interest in the space, or the sketches on the wall. She has a purpose.

I didn't ask him to come here, she says.

I know.

I don't know how he found out about you.

A picture, I suppose. We are the same.

You are not the same. He is good and kind.

He is rash and undisciplined. He is the son of his mother and does not think. I am smoking and I point at her with the burning cigarette as I speak. I was not angry when she appeared at my door, but it is rising now.

He should not have come. You will ruin him.

I think he will not come again.

He has no one else. It is the same as before. She wants but does not want.

He has you, I say.

She removes the scarf and shows me the future.

My work on the statue of Maggie progresses. I see her in it; it arouses me to touch her. But Maggie herself does not return. The boyfriend is back, she is pregnant, with his child, she says. It is no matter. We fucked. The work is nearly finished when Daniel appears.

He does not knock; he pushes the door open and he is just there, as if he has always been there. With the creation nearly finished, the pain of it is less intense. I am part of the world, I notice, and so I look up when he steps inside. His eyes are aflame. His face is thickly stubbled. The hair is longer than it was.

You are not my father, he says.

Look at you, I say. Who can deny it? What must his mother have thought watching such a boy grow.

I will do it this time.

I know he speaks of the statue of his mother, but I say, What do you mean?

He moves through the studio, again watching me, but this time it is not the shock of seeing himself grown old that holds him; he does not trust me. I hold the knife in my hand. He moves step by cautious step.

It is open space, there is no place to hide anything the size of the statue. He circles twice and each time comes back to the closet. There is no doubt. He knows. I wonder if I have remembered to lock it.

Leave. Now. You're a foolish boy and I have no time for fools.

He reaches to open the closet door, but it does not move.

Open it.

No.

I will not allow this image of my mother to exist.

It is not yours to decide, Daniel. Your mother.

My mother is dead.

The melodrama again. She isn't. I've seen her.

She died, old man. It was the end.

I'm sorry.

Bullshit! He kicks at the door but there is no movement. You killed her, he shouts. You didn't care about her, nobody cared. You bastard! The anger, the passion of his first visit has returned. He kicks the closet again, but nothing. And now he turns toward me once more and he seems enormous, swollen with fury and grief. The knife burns in my hand. But he is my son.

He steps toward me.

I ask, When?

Now. My whole life. Yesterday.

You're alone, I say.

You bastard. He steps.

The knife is in my hand.

He lunges and grabs my arm, twisting. He is strong. I cannot move my arm, my hand, and I would not if I could. I could not. I would not. The knife falls.

Open the door, he says.

Please, I say.

Open it.

Did I have a choice then? Do I now? I pull the key from my pocket and open the door. I stand before the covered statue, my arms spread.

Please, I say again.

He pushes me aside too easily and unshrouds his mother. She stands, naked, unashamed, welcoming what I have given her. He strikes, he pounds with his fists. He spies the mallet and he swings and swings and returns his mother to dust.

◆ ◆ ◆

Daniel is gone. He will never return, I'm sure of it. He will find his way in the world, or not. It is not my concern.

The statue of Maggie is finished and she waits, watching as I begin new work.

Smoke rolls from my lips and nose. It is birth, new life, that pours from my fingers. Now the head emerges, the ears, the wild eyes and sharp nose, the furious hands. Daniel rises from the clay and he is angry. He shouts, You bastard, you destroyed her, and he begs me to beat him, to punish him as myself. I beat the clay, I pound it, I beg its forgiveness, but it is not enough. He is me, but he is not me and there is more of me to put into him that I cannot. I see my fingers work the clay. I ply the knife to define him, to paint the anger in his face, to mold the flaring nose, and as I carve I see my fingers in the earth and I carve and take my hands away and still a finger rests in the child's belly, pointing, accusing, leaking life into the clay.

I drop the knife. I feel the flow, its warmth, and my hands return to the work, kneading, pushing, thrusting, thrusting the finger deeper inside him, burying my life inside the body of my son.

Maggie returns. I heard a scream, she says.

I have wrapped my hand in a foul rag that the blood has colored red, turning black. The girl lifts her hand to her mouth and turns away from the sight. I watch her swelling grace, notice the curve of her hip, how glistening sweat lines the creases of her neck. She sways as she hurries off, unable to stand the sight of me, and I wonder at the future of the child, what horrors have been set in motion for it, for the father, for her.

The door to her apartment closes. There is a soft echo in the hall. And then there is nothing. The studio is silent, with just the smoke from my cigarette enfolding the image of my son. I breathe in the smell of him, of us. I imagine his eyes, the creamy face, and I long for him. I imagine he is here, that I hold him in my arms. But there is nothing, there is only the dead clay, life buried in the earth, like a heart of stone.

WHAT THE ZHANG BOYS KNOW ABOUT LIFE ON PLANET EARTH

Simon is convinced that his mother will return. He knows it can happen. He learned about it in Sunday school. Sometimes God takes people to heaven and then lets them come back. He told his father this, but Baba just shook his head. When Ye-Ye, Baba's father, came from China to live with them, Simon explained it to him, even though Ye-Ye didn't speak English. He nodded, took Simon's hand, and pointed to the photograph of Simon's mother on the little table he'd made for the living room, with a candle that smelled like soap, some red and white flowers, and the pile of oranges that Wesley kept knocking over by accident.

Wesley, even though he's younger than Simon, knows more Chinese words because he gets to spend all day with Ye-Ye while Simon goes to school. Chinese is the English they speak in China, which is where Ye-Ye is from and also where Baba is from, but not Mama. Wesley calls Simon "Ge-Ge," which means Older Brother in Chinese. Sometimes it's easier for Wesley to say what he wants in Chinese because that's what Ye-Ye understands best. Like milk. Wesley showed Ye-Ye the bottle of milk and said, "milk," but Ye-Ye said, "*niu nai,*" so now that's what Wesley calls it. When Grandmother—

that's Mama's mother—came to visit, she raised her voice when Wesley called it that.

"It's milk," she said. "Why can't you say milk? Every child in America says milk. We're not in China, are we? Your mother said milk when she was a little girl and we're going to call it milk from now on."

Simon's skin tingles when Grandmother talks about Mama. Wesley still says, "*niu nai,*" but only with Ye-Ye.

Simon doesn't think much of Baba's new friend, Miss Lee. She doesn't look at all like Mama, who had yellow hair. Miss Lee looks like Baba, and like Ye-Ye, with a flat nose and black-black hair. Sometimes they go together in the car and come back after Simon and Wesley are supposed to be asleep. But Simon can't sleep, not since Mama's accident, and so he hears Baba and Miss Lee come into the living room and whisper. Wesley likes Miss Lee but Simon is afraid she will come to live with them, because then Mama will be angry and won't come back.

The Zhang boys are not supposed to play in the alley behind their building, but they do anyway. If their father is home, he will tell them they mustn't. But if he isn't home, or if he doesn't see, they pretend the alley is a river. If they run very fast they can cross without sinking, by stepping just on the top of the water, which is something else Simon learned about in Sunday school, but if they are too slow, the river will catch them and they will drown. Sometimes they find treasures in the river, like smelly old balloons and bits of shiny glass, and once Simon found a doctor's needle. He thought about playing doctor with the needle, to give Wesley a shot like the time Mama took them to the hospital when Wesley was really sick, but it looked dirty so instead he threw it in the garbage.

◆ ◆ ◆

Mr. Craig also lives in their building. He has a dog. It's a very small dog, which makes Simon happy. He has seen big dogs in the neighborhood, dogs as big as him, but he's afraid of those dogs. Sascha is a pug dog, and Baba says the reason he likes Sascha is that pugs originally came from China. Sascha has a squished face and a little tail that goes in a circle. Simon saw the dog poop once in the hallway and Mr. Craig told Simon not to tell anyone.

"Our little secret," he said, and gave Simon a piece of chocolate.

Mr. Craig lives in the same house with Mr. Charles, but Mr. Charles went away for a while and now he isn't feeling well, that's what Mr. Craig says, and he hardly ever comes outside.

There's a room in the basement that Mr. Artoyen keeps locked, and one time Simon saw Mr. Artoyen put some big boxes inside. He turned around and saw Simon standing there and he put his finger to his lips and said shh, and Simon didn't know why. Except now he really wants to know what's in those boxes.

Wesley didn't want to go to China with Baba and Simon, but Baba said it would be fun. Wesley admits that he did like the airplane, and he liked riding up to the top of the tower in Ye-Ye's hometown, but he thinks China smells bad, worse than the basement the time he found a dead rat there, and he doesn't ever want to go back. Also, people looked at him and he didn't understand what anyone said, even Ye-Ye. Baba took Simon for a walk along the river, but the sidewalk was too crowded. Once, he let go of Baba's hand and couldn't see him and suddenly everyone on the street looked like Baba. Simon started running and calling for Baba and someone grabbed him and he looked up and it was Baba, and after that he didn't let go of Baba's hand.

◆ ◆ ◆

Simon is tired of pretending the alley is a river. Anyway, except when it grows puddles after a rain, it looks more like a desert. Some other kids from the neighborhood visit his desert sometimes. One boy dribbled a basketball and let Simon try. The boy laughed at Simon, and Simon wanted to run back inside and tell the boy to stay out of his desert, but then the boy showed Simon how to do it, how to tap the ball with the ends of his fingers and let it come all the way back up and tap it again. They practiced running through the desert with the basketball and they laughed, but that time they were laughing *together* so it felt good. When the boy had to go home they shook hands. The boy's name is Eddie. He's black.

No one is supposed to know, but Miss Susanna has a cat. The cat's name is Tigger, which Simon thinks is funny because it's just a little cat. The cat used to live outside, but one day Miss Susanna gave it some smelly fish and it went inside with her. She lives in the first apartment, all by herself now that Mr. Thomas has gone away. Just her and Tigger. Simon sees Mr. Thomas sometimes, sitting in a car across the street from Nanking Mansion, just watching. Simon waves, but Mr. Thomas sinks down and pretends not to see.

Wesley says he wants to be a pilot when he grows up, but Simon thinks he might like to be an artist. He isn't sure what an artist does, exactly, but sometimes he watches Mr. Daniel make things with clay and that looks fun. One day nobody could find Wesley but it turned out he was sitting in Mr. Daniel's living room where he makes things and he was just watching. Mr. Daniel even gave him a lump of clay to play with, and a knife. But Baba grabbed the knife away from Wesley and told Simon to take Wesley home while he talked to Mr. Daniel. Simon and Wesley didn't hear what they said but when Baba came home he told the boys not to play with sharp things like knives. Simon didn't tell him about the needle he found, just in case that was one of the sharp things Baba was talking about. There's another artist in the building, Mr. Calvin, who paints pictures. Simon doesn't like his pictures much because they don't look like anything. They aren't like the pictures he draws in school of trees and houses and people. Baba put a picture Simon drew on the refrigerator with a magnet. It's a picture of Mama.

There's a man in the building who has no furniture. His name is hard to pronounce, like Baba and Ye-Ye's names, but he's not Chinese. He's black. He said to call him Mr. Al. One day Baba took the boys to Mr. Al's house because he had to go to work and there was no one to watch them. It was funny because there was no place to sit down and Mr. Al had a hole in his wall! It was like a window in his bedroom, but it was right in the brick wall and there was no glass or screen or anything. Simon felt a breeze and they all stuck their heads out and looked down at the alley. From there it looked like the moon, not a desert, except you could also see other buildings. Pigeons flew inside through the hole and they were walking around Mr. Al's bedroom! Simon and Wesley helped him get the pigeons to fly back outside.

"They belong outside," Mr. Al said, and Simon thought that was right, although he was sorry to see them go.

Sascha the pug ran away for a while but now he's back. There used to be two pugs living with Mr. Charles and Mr. Craig, but one of them ran away for good, which made Sascha sad, and also made Mr. Charles sad. Sascha ran away to look for his friend but he gave up and came home. Simon thinks Sascha might also have been looking for his mother, because Simon's been thinking he should do the same thing. He's trying to decide whether to tell Wesley about it, but he probably won't because Wesley might want to come with him and he's too little for something important like that.

Miss Susanna is getting fat. When Mr. Thomas was living in the front apartment with her they used to fight. Simon heard them. Sometimes he and Wesley would have races in the hallway and then they would stand outside the door of some of the apartments and listen to the people inside. Mr. Thomas was very loud. But other times there were different noises inside their apartment and Simon wasn't sure what was happening because there were no words, exactly. Wesley noticed that when Miss Susanna and Mr. Thomas were together in the hallway or outside they were always touching each other, or holding hands like Baba would hold his hand when they walked down the street. But sometimes Miss Susanna looked at Mr. Thomas with her eyes open wide, like she was about to cry.

Eddie has an older friend—Simon thinks he might be Eddie's brother but he isn't sure—who is mean to him. Simon told Baba that the older boy hit Eddie and yelled at him, but Baba said they couldn't do anything about it.

"It's their family," he said. "We can only take care of our own family."

But Simon is afraid of Eddie's brother.

Simon thinks someday he'd like to visit Mars. In school they learned about the planets, how some of them far, far away are too cold and everything there is frozen, and some of them get too close to the sun and so the people there had to leave because it was too hot. But it might be okay to live on Mars. No one knows for sure.

To get to Mars, Simon would need a spaceship. Baba took him and Wesley to a museum where they had a spaceship and also some airplanes. When Simon and Wesley and Baba went in an airplane to China to bring Ye-Ye back to Nanking Mansion to live with them, the airplane was as big as the spaceship in the museum. Simon wanted to ask the pilot if they could go to Mars instead of China, but he walked up and down the aisles and up the stairs and couldn't find the pilot. He did look out the window at the stars, though. He couldn't see Mars. He wonders if heaven is on Mars and if that's where his mother went.

Baba says that Miss Susanna is going to have a baby. Miss Susanna has gotten really fat and Simon guesses that fat people have babies, and he wonders if Mr. Artoyen is also going to have a baby. Simon remembers when Wesley was born. He doesn't really remember, but Baba has shown him pictures of Mama before Wesley came. She was fat. Simon does remember lying in bed at night listening to Mama read a story about the moon and he remembers that she smelled like flowers.

Simon has been learning to tell time. Baba gave him a watch and Simon likes to wear it to school and tell the other kids what time it is and he also wears it around the neighborhood. He showed it to Eddie and explained about the hands and the numbers. But then Eddie's brother came and took Simon's watch. This happened yesterday and Simon is afraid to tell Baba. So he holds his wrist behind his back or pulls his sleeve down really far, which pulls it up on the other side.

Simon has an idea how to get his watch back. Mr. Al, the man with the hole in his wall, is black. Eddie and his brother are black. So maybe Mr. Al knows them and he can ask to get it back. Simon knocks on Mr. Al's door and Mr. Al smiles and invites him in. There is no place to sit because he still has no furniture. Simon wonders if the hole is still there, but he thinks he shouldn't ask, even though he and Mr. Al are friends and Mama said you can ask your friend anything. He explains about the watch and Mr. Al nods.

"Do you know where Eddie and his brother live?" asks Mr. Al.

Simon is sorry to say that he does not. He wishes he did, because that's probably where the watch is, too. But it doesn't seem to bother Mr. Al, who grabs his coat out of his closet. They go out behind the building and Simon starts to explain how the alley used to be a river but now it's a desert. Or the moon.

He hears the boing-boing of Eddie's basketball, not in the alley but somewhere nearby. He and Mr. Al stand in the alley and Simon hears the ball coming closer. He hears voices, too, Eddie and Eddie's brother. Simon takes Mr. Al's hand.

"What's up, Chinaboy?" Eddie's brother says.

"That's not a very nice thing to say," Mr. Al says. "Apologize to the boy."

The voice he uses isn't mean really, but it is kind of strict, like the teachers at school, and Simon is surprised when Eddie's brother stands up a little straighter and looks Mr. Al in the eye. Simon sees his watch on Eddie's brother's wrist at just the same time Mr. Al says, "That the boy's watch?"

"The kid gave it to me," says Eddie's brother.

"That's not the way I heard it," says Mr. Al, and in the end Eddie's brother takes off the watch and gives it back to Simon, but he doesn't look happy about it.

China is on the other side of Earth. At school the teacher showed Simon a globe and pointed to China, a big red spot that looked hot, but Simon remembers that it wasn't hot at all. The teacher took a piece of string and taped it to the spot he called Washington and they measured the distance to China going one way and it was 9 inches and then they measured going the other way and it was the same. Simon likes the food in Washington better, like hot dogs, but he liked some things in China, too, like fried dumplings, and now that Ye-Ye lives with them he cooks some of those things. Mama was a good cook. She used to make spaghetti and sometimes when Simon was sick she would let him eat pudding in bed.

Miss Claudia is another woman who lives in the building but she doesn't let Simon and Wesley come inside her apartment. She's been getting skinnier and skinnier. After Simon told Baba that she might be sick, Baba took her some oranges.

Simon has seen Miss Susanna go inside Mr. Daniel's apartment and he's also seen her go inside Mr. Calvin's apartment and sometimes she stays for a long time.

Sometimes Simon goes down into the basement to see if Mr. Artoyen forgot to lock the door on that room with the boxes, but so far he never has. Wesley won't come with him. He's afraid of the basement.

Mr. Craig has another friend besides Mr. Charles. One day when Sascha got away Baba and Simon and Wesley brought him back to Mr. Craig's apartment and at the same time another man came right behind them. Mr. Craig was surprised, like the man had gone to heaven and come back, and Simon wanted to ask the man if he knew Mama. Simon has seen Mr. Craig come out of his apartment and meet the new man on the sidewalk or in his car and they go off together. Mr. Craig told Simon not to tell Mr. Charles and he gave him some more chocolate.

One time when Ye-Ye was sick and Baba had to take him to the hospital, Miss Lee came over to stay with Simon and Wesley. Wesley likes Miss Lee because she is the only one who will play the games that he likes with his cards that he doesn't understand anyway. He makes up the rules or he just doesn't use any rules at all and Simon thinks the real rules make the game better so he doesn't like to play those games with Wesley. But Miss Lee doesn't care. When it was dark and they'd had their dinner and Baba had not come home with Ye-Ye yet, Miss Lee told them it was time for bed.

Simon said, "You're not my mother."

Miss Lee was quiet and then said, "No, I'm not." She looked like she might cry and then she said, "But you have to go to bed anyway." She read them that story about the moon.

Simon heard Baba come home late that night, but Ye-Ye didn't come home for a few days and when he did come home he didn't move around very well and everyone had to be quiet while he rested. Baba stayed home from work to take care of him and he made tea and soup. But then Ye-Ye was okay again and Simon thought he was happy to have someone to take care of him because back in China he didn't have anyone.

After that, Simon got to thinking that it would be very nice if Mama came home so Miss Lee wouldn't have to come over any more and so they'd all have someone to take care of them if they got sick. Sometimes he looks at the picture of Mama on the little table so he won't forget what she looks like. The picture was taken in the park when they went there to play on the swings, and Mama's hair is blowing because of the wind and she's laughing and the sun is bright in her eyes. There's another picture on that table and Ye-Ye says that's Nai-Nai, Baba's mother, and so Simon got to thinking that if he could find Mama he might also find Nai-Nai and they could both come to live in the house and Ye-Ye would be happy again.

Finally, Simon decides it's time to go look for Mama, and when he slips out the front door, as quietly as he can because he doesn't want Ye-Ye to know he's gone, Wesley sees him.

"Where are you going, Ge-Ge?" Wesley asks.

Simon says "Shh," takes Wesley's hand, and pulls him out the door. "I'm going to find Mama," he says, and when he does a big grin pops up on Wesley's face and then there is no way to keep him at home.

They start in the alley, which is now the moon, and isn't the moon a planet like Mars? He's never gone to the end of the alley because Baba told him he shouldn't, but now he does because otherwise they'll never find Mama. When he gets to the end, it isn't the moon anymore, it's just a gray street like the street in front of Nanking Mansion and he decides to go down the hill because it's easier but also because if they go up the hill it just takes them back to their own street. So down the hill they go.

Simon sees Mr. Craig and his new friend holding hands, just like he is holding Wesley's hand now. He doesn't want to talk to Mr. Craig because Mr. Craig will tell him to go home, so he turns another corner.

He sees Eddie bouncing his basketball but he doesn't want to talk to Eddie either, and he especially doesn't want to talk to Eddie's brother now that he has his watch back, so he pulls Wesley the other way and they turn another corner.

And now he isn't sure where they are. It's a street just like the street they live on but he doesn't see any houses that look familiar and he doesn't see any people he can ask and he's afraid to go up the steps to one of the houses to ring the doorbell. If they keep walking he thinks he'll recognize something sooner or later and anyway going someplace new was the point because he's supposed to be on his way to find Mama.

So they keep walking and nothing looks right and Simon is beginning to think he's made a mistake. They come to a busy street with cars rushing both ways and trucks and it's noisy. He has learned about crossing streets, though, so he holds Wesley's hand as they stand at the corner and wait for the cars to stop. Except they don't stop and he wonders if he's forgotten something about when they stop, and while he's wondering that a long green bus pulls up at the corner. He thinks now is when he's supposed to cross the street but it's only the bus that has stopped. The cars still rush by and he grips Wesley's hand a little harder. Wesley isn't saying anything, which Simon knows means he's afraid, and sometimes when Wesley is afraid Simon likes to make fun of him but not this time. The door to the bus whooshes open, which makes Simon jump back just a little, and he peeks inside. He wonders if he should get on the bus, if that would be the way to find Mama, but the bus is full of people and the bus driver looks at him, and when Simon doesn't move he closes the door and the bus pulls away in a cloud, like it's blasting off for Mars.

When the bus is gone Simon realizes that the cars have stopped and just then a woman starts crossing the street from the opposite direction, so Simon steps off the curb. He has to tug on Wesley's arm to get him to come along, but the two of them make it across the street before the traffic begins again. Simon feels lighter now, like he's done something important and has one less thing to worry about as he searches for Mama, so he turns to Wesley and grins. Wesley grins back, but Simon isn't sure that Wesley understands what they have just done and how important it is.

On the other side of the street there is a small park: a triangle of flowers, shrubs and small trees, and some benches. Simon picks a bench that isn't too dirty and he and Wesley sit. Simon wants to think about what to do next. He wishes he could ask his friend Mr. Al for advice and he decides if he can't find Mama today that the next time he goes looking for her he will ask Mr. Al. He also wishes he had brought some food because his stomach is rumbly and he's pretty sure that astronauts on their way to Mars would take some sandwiches or an apple.

Wesley fidgets like he has to go to the bathroom and Simon is beginning to understand that this search isn't such a good idea.

A woman walks by with a little dog on a leash. The little dog is about the size of a pug, but has long hair and a sparkly collar. The dog comes over to the bench and sniffs at Simon's feet. Wesley pulls his feet up on the bench. He's not afraid of dogs, but he doesn't like to be sniffed.

"Hello," says the woman, and Simon says hello back.

"Are you lost?" she asks.

"No," Simon answers while Wesley nods. "We're looking for our mother."

"And where is she?"

"She might be on Mars," Simon says, "or at least that's what I think."

The woman smiles but doesn't say anything.

"Do you know how to get there?" Simon asks.

The woman looks at him and Simon notices that she smells sweet, like one of those pages from Mama's magazines.

"No, I don't believe I do," the woman says. "But I'm sure a bus will be along any minute." And then she yanks on the little dog's leash and the two of them walk away.

When she's gone, Wesley says, "I'm hungry," and makes little squeaking noises like he's about to cry.

Simon doesn't want to tell Wesley that he's hungry, too. He wants to tell him to be quiet and not to cry, but he's afraid that if he does Wesley will cry for real. It's beginning to get dark and some of the cars have their lights on. Now there are more people on the sidewalk, too. It reminds Simon of being in China and he feels like he did when he let go of his father's hand and couldn't see him any more. Wesley moves closer to Simon and Simon takes his hand.

"Simon!"

He looks up to see where his name is coming from because he thinks his mother is calling to him. Mama has found them and he was right all along!

But it isn't his mother. It's Miss Lee. She's in a little white car on the street and she's leaning out the window and then she's opening the door and running across the grass and jumping over the flowers and the bushes and she wraps her arms around Wesley and Simon.

"We were so worried," she says. "Your father came home and you were gone and we've been looking everywhere. What were you thinking?"

Simon wants to tell her what he was thinking, even though he knows she might be angry.

Miss Lee starts to cry and that makes Wesley cry harder, and even Simon is sniffling. More than ever, he wishes Mama were here, to take him home to Nanking Mansion, to cook dinner for their family, to tell him stories, to bring him pudding in bed and talk to him about all the things he doesn't understand. But she isn't there, and for the first time since the accident he thinks maybe she isn't coming back. Maybe, just maybe, he and Wesley are going to have to find their own way, without their mother, across all the streets and rivers and deserts in the world.

HUNGER

Claudia pulls the *zabuton* from the armoire and arranges the cushion squarely in the center of the *tatami* mat she and Timothy brought home from the Zen retreat that was their honeymoon. She lights incense and dims the overhead fixture. She was taught to meditate while listening to recordings of natural sounds—the rushing of a stream, the twitter of birds—as if those reproductions were somehow more real than anything else she might hear, like honking horns, or a clattering subway. But she prefers actual music, with manmade instruments and transformative melodies that soar and take her with them. So now it is the Bach suites for cello pouring from her Bose speakers, and she prepares to fly.

She adjusts her leotard, pulling it free from where it has crept into awkward crevices, stretches momentarily, fingertips to toes and side to side, and descends onto the cushion. She folds her legs, places hands on knees, straightens her back, breathes deeply, and closes her eyes.

This much is right, she knows, having progressed that far in the retreat. Timothy had stuck it out for the whole week, an accomplishment about which he boasted for months, but she had been restless from the moment her eyes closed and a disembodied, amplified voice instructed the group to breathe and look into the nothingness. What nonsense! There had been nothing there to look at, and somehow that was supposed to be the point. And she couldn't very well *not* breathe, could she? Absurd. She'd slipped away, not unnoticed, and set out exploring Kyoto's landmarks: The Temple of the Golden Pavilion, The Silver Pagoda, the Palace. And the rest of the week she'd shopped. That was her kind of meditation.

But times have changed. This is Washington, D.C., not Kyoto. Timothy is gone and her job along with him. She's still restless, but there will be no shopping. Not since her debt counselor had snipped all of her credit cards in half at their first session. Not since her third bounced check. Not since the notice from the nice people at Countrywide that her mortgage payment was overdue. As if she didn't know. She had mentioned to the counselor, as a way of avoiding the painful subject at hand, that she'd made a brief stab at meditation years ago, and the woman pounced, insisted that Claudia should give it another try. It could help control the spending urges, she'd claimed, and, if nothing else, might help Claudia see her diminished circumstances in a new and hopeful light.

And so the eyes are closed. She counts her breaths. She lets the blackness overtake her, tries to see nothing, not even the spiraling point of light that seems to be coming directly toward her. It is far in the distance, like a ship on the horizon, but its movement is perceptible. She begins again to count her breaths, but the more she tries not to see the point of light, the closer it seems, and the faster it moves, until she fears it will slice into her. At the last moment before the inevitable impact, she opens her eyes.

She assumes the point of light has something to do with hunger. She has not eaten today and has no recollection of having eaten since the day before yesterday, or possibly the day before that, when Mr. Zhang, the kindly widower at the end of the hall, brought a plate of tangerines to her door in celebration of some Asian holiday. It was his little boys who handed her the fruit, she remembers now, offering a greeting that sounded well-rehearsed, in a language she didn't understand.

In the darkness before her eyes she now imagines the boys' return. They have knocked on the door and she has welcomed them in. "We brought dinner," says Simon, the older boy. He presents her with a bowl, steam curling from a thick, pungent broth. The image—the boys, the soup—is a figment, of course, and yet her mouth waters in anticipation. "Noodles," says the little one, Wesley. She devours the noodles with chopsticks, although in fact she has never mastered their use, and she slurps the broth. She lifts bites of tender beef to her mouth, bitter greens, sharp peppers. "Delicious," she says, the tang of ginger on her tongue. And when the soup is finished, the boys vanish in the darkness.

Claudia loves children and wishes she and Timothy had had at least one, but of course under the circumstances it is a blessing they didn't. A child would have made the divorce that much more difficult, and if there were children to consider, what would she do now? It's bad enough as it is, but she isn't the kind of woman who begs help from the government, even to feed a child. She has no idea how food stamps work, or if food stamps even survived Clinton's "welfare reform." Where do people turn for help these days? As for Timothy, that's another long sad story.

Their split had been mostly amicable, in large part because there were so few assets to fight over: the condo and the furniture, the carpets, the treasured Japanese woodblock prints they brought back from Kyoto. Timothy, in any case, in pursuit of some outlandishly ascetic ideal, had wanted none of it. He just wanted to be free. They'd come to know each other when she fled the corporate prison that was Burson-Marsteller to work her public relations magic for his tiny healthcare consulting firm. That had led to romance—not earth-moving romance, certainly, but still it was a pleasant disruption. At her age, Claudia no longer expected to set the world aflame, or find her one true love, or achieve world peace. A nice life was enough, and that's what Timothy had offered.

They had only been married a couple of years when Timothy decided it was a mistake, that he needed his own space, that he couldn't begin to change for Claudia, or any woman for that matter, and wouldn't dream of asking her to adjust to him either, even if she might be willing. The more he thought about it, he'd told her, the more he realized he didn't love her, was probably incapable of love, and the clearer it became that he had to leave. There had been no discussion, no argument. Claudia couldn't say Timothy was wrong, because she knew he wasn't. In the settlement, she'd taken the apartment, nominally theirs by virtue of the barest down payment, along with the mortgage, and Timothy took the car, his Toyota, in which, Claudia had discovered recently, he now lives.

Which would have been fine—humiliating and disappointing, but fine—because, having settled for less once, she could give herself permission to settle for less again, even less than the first time, if necessary. But Timothy had decided that not only was he incapable of love, he was also incapable of running a business. He'd rolled up the office like a cheap rug, cancelled contracts, fired staff, returned the leased furniture and equipment to Rent-A-Center, and called the consulting firm quits as well. Having left a secure, if suffocating, job for the freedom and challenge Timothy had promised, Claudia hadn't known if she could go back.

She's been hunting for something else, a position offering pay and status commensurate with her age and experience, but so far, after six months, has landed nothing. Now the mortgage payment is overdue, and the electricity will stop flowing at any moment, taking with it the phone, if by then it, too, has not already been shut off.

She realizes she has slumped on her *zabuton*; she straightens her back, returns her hands to their proper position, and shuts her eyes again. The blackness now spins, although possibly it is her body that sways from exhaustion and hunger and, perhaps, fear of what the future holds. The spinning blackness reveals moments of light and dark, and in the light, in strobe-like flashes, she sees a face. It is her own face—an attractive woman nearing middle-age, her hair frosted and cut short for an active lifestyle—and she is seated in the lotus position with her eyes closed. At first Claudia thinks it is her sister Daphne. They have the same features and coloring, and it wasn't unheard of when they were growing up in Cleveland for one to be mistaken for the other, although Claudia was already away at college when Daphne began high school. But Daphne lives in fast-paced L.A. and, as far as Claudia knows, wouldn't be caught dead meditating. In fact, the woman she sees in the moments of light is seated in Claudia's own living room, except that the room is bare. There is no furniture, no artwork. There are no rugs. There is only the woman on the meditation cushion in the center of the room.

Claudia opens her eyes and the first thing she sees is the Hiroshige print from the Tokaido series.

In the back room of a gallery in Kalorama, Claudia unwraps three framed woodblock prints. The art dealer—an aging queen she and Timothy consulted once on a prospective purchase that, fortunately, they decided not to make—seems happy to have the Hiroshige and the Hokusai, both of which date from the 1830s and are in fine condition.

"But this one," he says with a dismissive sneer at the

Toyokuni, which suffers from a single, barely noticeable wormhole, "is hopeless."

If she were adept at haggling, none of this would be necessary. She would have wrung more out of Timothy, or she would have found a job already, and she would never have been forced to sell these objects she adores. But she's hungry, and there is no money.

"It's a package deal," she says. She stumbles over the words and has to repeat them, fearing that the dealer has not heard.

He studies the print, which depicts a white-faced Kabuki actor gazing at his reflection in a mirror, and sighs. He holds it under a lamp, points to the wormhole, and sighs again.

"There are other dealers," says Claudia, surprised by her own persistence. She moves to rewrap the prints, and the dealer raises his fleshy hand.

"I know I'll regret this," he says, pulling a ledger from an antique writing desk. He signs a generous check with a rococo flourish, flapping it in the air to dry the ink, and surrenders it to Claudia with a deep bow.

Outside, she allows herself to breathe. She has a vague notion of what Timothy paid for the prints at the gallery in Kyoto, so she considers the price fair. It will, in any case, buy groceries. She has already identified other possessions she can sell if it comes to that: her armoire is French provincial, and should cover a month or two of her mortgage; she and Timothy collected Persian tribal rugs and those should fetch a decent sum, although the market for rugs is notoriously fickle; she has rings and earrings and bracelets, some of which are set with semi-precious stones; there's the custom-made bicycle she bought in a deluded moment of eco-enthusiasm; even the designer couch must be worth something.

She continues to check the job listings on Monster.com and she scours the *Washington Post*. She submits her résumé, slightly exaggerated, for only perfect jobs: those with a suitable title and salary. She has standards, a reputation. At her age she isn't about to start at the bottom again, although those are the jobs that are most plentiful. There are few jobs that approach her ideal. A respected boutique marketing-communications firm with an office in Chevy Chase invites her for an interview. Although she dreads the commute on the Metro, at least it wouldn't involve driving in city traffic she hates in a car she doesn't own, and so she keeps the appointment.

She meets with an account manager, who appears to be fresh from college, and understands that she's being screened by a low-level staff member. If she isn't deemed worthy she will make it no further than this.

"Why would you leave Burson?" he asks. "Isn't that marketing heaven?"

"It's a fine firm, of course," she says. "I simply thought it was time to try something new. Something with more responsibility." That's what he wants to hear, isn't it? That she has initiative?

Her interviewer excuses himself—to report to higher-ups, presumably—and while he is gone she tries to picture herself in his office. The firm isn't as bloated and deadly as her old company, but it *is* busy and solid and looks as if it expects to be around for a while. This will work. This will allow her to right her sinking ship, get her bearings. She looks forward to meeting the rest of the hiring team, the bosses, even settling into an office or a cubicle of her own, finding a nice plant for her desk, building a personal space, growing accustomed to the commute. The interviewer returns.

"We'll be in touch," he says, and then adds something about demographics and diversity. "Thanks for coming in."

Claudia knows she'll never hear from them.

Her next interview is in Arlington, also a Metro trek, but doable. As she dresses she notices that the suit she's chosen for the meeting is loose. It hangs on her because of the weight she's lost, what with the economizing she's been doing and the worry over where her life is headed, and she can see that elsewhere, too: in her drawn face, the drooping skin on her arms and legs. She needs to have the outfit taken in, but there's no time for that now. She arrives at Arlington's Courthouse Square, an unattractive hodge-podge of classical and post-modern low-rise buildings, and finds the suite of offices. It's another boutique outfit, but this time she's kept occupied for several hours, meeting half a dozen people. It's like any office: a couple of her prospective co-workers are losers who are destined to be pushed out, but there's a sharp woman in a crisp, charcoal suit who is clearly a superstar and an exceedingly attractive man who at least pretties up the place. At the end of the grueling day it is the leader of the team, the woman Claudia has identified as the go-getter, who tells her it's a no-go. We'll keep your application on file, she says, but you're not quite what we're looking for right now.

The next week she's called to a small firm in Georgetown near the canal. The location is outstanding, just below busy M Street, and she's determined to make this interview count. It's a long four blocks from the Foggy Bottom Metro station, so she has to speed-walk to avoid being late. As it is, she's out of breath when she announces herself to the receptionist, mortified to give such a first impression, and hopes that this place isn't the sort that allows clerical staff a say in hiring decisions. She meets with three people in a small conference room, each clutching a copy of her résumé, and answers questions about her education, experience, and specialties. That group leaves the room and another comes in, peppering her with specific questions about projects she's identified on her CV as exemplary and about the kind of work she'd like to do in her next position. The final group of three, including the hiring manager, asks about her availability, her salary requirements, and her willingness to travel. It all seems so promising and pointed, as if the decision is already made and the offer merely a formality, that she allows herself to think that this time it will work out. The crisis is over. The hunger she has suppressed re-emerges, like a snake drawn forth by the promise of spring. She is left alone and closes her eyes, breathes deeply, searches for the moment of light.

She opens her eyes when she senses she's no longer alone. The hiring manager is smiling, extending her hand. Thank you for coming, we all enjoyed meeting you, we just have some internal procedures to deal with and then we'll be in touch.

We'll be in touch. She's heard that before, but from this woman's mouth the words sound sincere. She doesn't feel like she's being given the brush-off. This one is it.

She goes home to wait.

The bills have begun to pile up again. Her artwork is depleted and she's sold most of the jewelry and antiques, including the armoire. She's working her way through the rugs, hoping she can hang on to her favorite Isfahan, but after that it gets more difficult— the books won't raise much cash, and selling the living room furniture would seem so final. Maybe she could sell the condo, but the equity wouldn't cover an agent's cut. She hasn't heard yet from the firm in Georgetown and is hesitant to call. With each day that passes, she interprets the silence differently: one moment she is certain the job is hers; the next she realizes she is delusional.

She still has the *zabuton* and meditates regularly now. Since she's given up her expensive wine habit, she considers meditation a substitute, and more refreshing. She sits in the center of the room. She isn't naked, but she might as well be, the way the leotard, even the normally skin-tight leotard, feels like an empty sack. The room is nearly empty, just the couch and the rug, a battered coffee table. She closes her eyes, counts her breaths, searches the dark, and in the distance sees the point of light. The light grows, moves closer, and again she sees a face. This time she thinks it is her own face but then, only when the jewelry sparkles around the neck and on each ear, realizes it's her sister. If Claudia owned such pieces she would have sold them by now. In fact, though, the glittering style is Daphne's, not hers.

Claudia doesn't see Daphne often. Since their parents' death there are no family gatherings, and Claudia, especially in the past few years, does not travel. Daphne's real estate work in Los Angeles keeps her tethered there. She has no children to care for, no husband, but she has clients, deals, always loose ends that need tending. They speak on the phone annually, on one or the other's birthday, generally not both. And they email from time to time.

Does she have a choice? She had shed her friends when she went to work for Timothy; it's been too long now. There is only Daphne. It isn't a conversation she wants to have. If her parents were alive, that's who she'd call. They'd had little themselves, both from working-class families, but would always help when Claudia asked, which she did when she was younger. Expenses in college, an occasional emergency when she was single, a "loan" from time to time when she was struggling. Even if her father resisted, on the grounds that Claudia was a big girl and could take care of herself, her mother could be counted on to send something. When they died, in rapid succession, Daphne, the proven businesswoman, the successful one, executed the estate. There wasn't much—the sisters split about a hundred thousand dollars, all from equity in the house—but pursuant to their father's instructions Claudia's share was reduced by the amount of the several loans, of which he'd kept meticulous account. The piddling sum that was left, a few thousand, is long gone. Daphne's share, Claudia is certain, was invested, saved, put to work, doubled by now, tripled. Daphne has money. She can help.

There is one other option, and Claudia considers how she might go about it. A colleague at Burson-Marsteller did it with pills, more a cry for help that went unheard, Claudia thinks, than a decisive act. Still, it did the trick. She owns a set of Henckles kitchen knives that she hasn't yet sold, but that involves pain, and a horrific mess. Same with a gun, if she could even find one. That, she concludes, would take more courage than she's ever demonstrated before. Drowning is an option, as there are plenty of bridges in the area and easy access to rivers or the ocean. It would be like meditation, wouldn't it? The eyes close, you sink in the darkness, looking for the moment of light. Eventually it comes, or not, and by that time it no longer matters. She shuts her eyes once more, imagines being swallowed by the water, and Daphne's face appears again.

Claudia rises unsteadily and lets her hand move to the phone, settling there slowly like a falling leaf, and picks it up to dial.

And then she changes her mind. An email would be better. She composes it while she stands with the phone in her hand. It's been harder than she expected to get a job. She's got résumés out, interviews pending, one offer expected at any moment (or at least possible; she no longer expects to hear from the people in Georgetown, but Daphne doesn't need to know that). She's got feelers out for freelance work and that looks promising. Very promising. But at the moment she's got a short-term cash flow problem. Could Daphne lend her a few thousand? Five, say? She opens her laptop, the one possession she can't do without if she's ever to make it out of this morass, types up the note, lets her finger hover over the 'send' key, and hits 'delete' instead. She starts again. In the end, though, it is virtually unchanged—what else is there to say?—and she lets it go.

Daphne's response, which Claudia sees the next morning after a sleepless night, is cryptic. Sure. Check's in the mail.

It's absurd, but Claudia brushes tears from her eyes. Daphne is her little sister and she's done well enough for herself that she can do this without batting an eye, as if five grand is nothing. Perhaps it is nothing for her, less than the commission on a small sale—a tiny sale in the L.A. market.

She can stall her bank for a few days until the check comes in, she can pay a bit on her credit card debt as her counselor advised. The homeowners' dues to the condo association can wait, but the electric company cannot. In an instant, in her mind, the money is spent, and she realizes she should have asked for more. But with renewed determination, her burden eased, she works on her résumé, looks at the job postings, even checks the internet for more far-flung opportunities. Paris would be fun. She enjoyed Japan. Even L.A. would be a nice change.

The check's in the mail. Good news, certainly, but in the mail isn't the same as in the bank, and in the meantime Claudia needs to eat.

On Seventh Street, near New Jersey Avenue, is a diner she's passed often but never entered. She goes there now, taking her time, the one commodity she has in abundance. When she arrives, she slides into a booth, a red vinyl that feels unclean and sticky, and studies the menu. She orders apple pie and coffee and she savors each bite, picks up the last crumbs from the plate with her fingers. When it's time to pay, she signals for the waitress, who comes bearing the coffee pot.

"I'm sorry," Claudia says in a whisper that the waitress has to bend forward to hear. "I seem to have left my wallet at home."

The waitress, a wide-hipped woman with skin the color of an old penny, doesn't say a word, doesn't blink.

"I'm so embarrassed. It's never happened before. I'll go home and come right back with the money. I swear."

The waitress stares into Claudia's eyes, shakes her head and clucks, piles the coffee cup on the pie plate and snatches them both off the table without a word. Claudia knows the woman doesn't believe her, that she's heard it all before, and has no doubt that she'll never see the money. She can't be bothered to make a fuss over a lousy slice of pie, and that's what Claudia was counting on. She feels guilty, of course, but what else can she do?

Three days go by and Daphne's check doesn't arrive. Each day Claudia pulls the same stunt in a different diner, with similar results, although one waitress, a dwarfish woman with a thick Spanish accent, follows her out of the restaurant as she flees and shouts something Claudia doesn't understand. But when on the fourth day the mail comes and she recognizes her sister's handwriting on a standard business envelope, it isn't relief that Claudia feels. She knows what the check represents, and what cashing it will cost her. She opens the envelope and finds Daphne's check, secure inside a sheet of her agency's letterhead, blank on both sides. Claudia looks for a note, but the envelope is empty.

She does not return to the diners to make good on her promise of payment. She's not out of the woods yet, and she knows it. Instead, she shops for specials in the supermarket: day-old bread, dairy on the cusp of expiration. She lingers briefly in the wine aisle, but if all she can afford is rotgut, then it's better to do without. She resolves to stick with the meditation.

She sends out more résumés. She goes on more interviews. But weeks pass and there is no job. The money is gone.

She again emails Daphne. This time it takes a day to get a response, but the answer is the same: cryptic, no questions, nothing. In four days the check arrives. The pattern repeats itself, month after month, although Claudia's reports to Daphne about her job-hunting efforts become more elaborately inflated, the account of her cost-cutting measures more detailed. Daphne hasn't asked for these reports, but Claudia feels obligated just the same. What else does she have to offer in return for the money?

Some of Claudia's attempts to land freelance work do bear fruit. She helps a small financial consulting firm with the content for their website and writes a brochure for a private religious school in the suburbs. She discovers that she has priced her work too low, considering the amount of time required to learn the respective businesses and to revise her work after initial input from the clients. She also discovers one of the perils of freelancing: the consulting firm is slow to pay, in part to manage their float but also because there are questions about whether Claudia's work is original (indeed, she has borrowed liberally from information she found on the internet, but she has no idea how the client might have discovered her petty plagiarism); and the school doesn't pay at all, despite repeated reminders.

It is now the sixth month of Claudia's nightmare, as she thinks of her predicament, and her ascetic mode of living has become almost normal. She has dropped her subscriptions to magazines and newspapers, her membership to the gym, her cable services, her cell phone. She has trimmed her landline service so that she now has only the basic access: no caller i.d., no call-waiting. It had long been her habit to visit Olsson's Bookstore on Seventh Street each week and, invariably, to come home with one or two of the latest hardcover releases. But she now can't enter the store, because the temptation is so great and because the pain of being unable to possess the books she wants drives deep into her soul. On her last visit she had tucked a slim novel under her sweater, setting off the alarms as she exited. She apologized for her absent-mindedness to the sales clerk, a Chinese girl who looked familiar, said she simply forgot to pay, and then in a fever of deep humiliation used all of her remaining cash to buy the book. She can't let that happen again. In fact, she has found ways to dispose of the books she already owns, by taking them to one of the used bookstores in DuPont Circle, or offering them for sale on eBay or Amazon, creating a trickle of income.

One of her freelance gigs is contract work for a minuscule marketing firm with an office in a redeveloped department store on Sixth Street. Because it is so close to her condo, she has met the principals, a husband-and-wife team, on two occasions, and, when her assignment is completed—she assisted with writing the annual report for a family planning non-profit—they offer her a salaried job. The money isn't great (by her calculations, it pays little more than the barista job she saw listed for a Starbucks), but there are benefits and, because she could walk to work, she would have zero additional expenses. As her new bosses provide details over espresso in their glass-and-steel conference room, her knees shake and she ignores the steaming cup before her so that they will not notice her trembling hands. She can barely speak, but she takes the job.

Her fingers tapping lightly across the laptop's keyboard, she sends a cheery email to Daphne with the good news, although she also has to ask for one last loan because it will be weeks before her first paycheck, and because she will need a few things for the new job. In fact what she needs is a whole new wardrobe, since she has sold a number of the more valuable items in her closet, and what is left is far too large for her diminished figure. She has already made an appointment with a dressmaker to have several outfits altered, but she will need to buy new, as well. Daphne responds immediately: Wonderful news, check in the mail.

Except the check doesn't arrive.

Claudia begins work and instantly clashes with the principals, especially the wife.

"You aren't to speak with the client," says the wife on Claudia's second day, after she has called a vice president in the company for whom she is writing copy for a new brochure.

"How am I supposed to get the information for the job?" Claudia asks.

"You come to me. Always come to me."

Although Claudia is older and far more experienced, the wife insists on her own way of doing things. Her editing of Claudia's work is excessive. She insists that personal items should not be left on desks overnight or when clients are present. She decrees that Claudia's skirt, for which Claudia has spent money she cannot spare, is too short. On the fourth day of her new job, Claudia calls in sick. She does, in fact, have a monumental headache that doesn't surprise her in the least, and her stomach churns its own rebellion. On the fifth day she begins an email that takes all day to write, in which she tenders her resignation.

An email arrives from Daphne. She apologizes for not sending the check, but she's made plans to come to Washington for a realtors' conference and she thought they should get together; she's looking forward to seeing her big sister.

It isn't panic that courses through Claudia, exactly, but more like a rumbling of dread, a foreboding of catastrophe. Daphne won't lend her the money, will see how Claudia's been living. She'll have to admit that she quit the job that was supposed to rescue her, and Daphne will be furious. There will be a scene, lectures, such as they heard endlessly from their father, about foolishness, about responsibility. She closes her eyes, feels herself succumbing to the deep water, being swallowed by the darkness.

There is one bright spot. Daphne has not asked to stay with Claudia. If she did, Claudia would have to identify a deterrent, the loud neighbor boys, perhaps (although, in truth, she finds them both perfectly charming, and their father and grandfather kind gentlemen); another neighbor's constant smoking; the unremitting smell of paint from the resident artists. But the conference Daphne's attending is at the Capitol Hilton and that's where she's staying.

"I want to see your place," she says over the phone, upon arrival, "but I don't know if there'll be time."

More relief. Daphne's flight from the coast was delayed and it's now late Thursday, too late to meet. She wants to take Claudia to dinner while she's in town, but she's decided to catch a late flight back on Saturday in order to make showings on Sunday that she can't afford to miss. So it's Friday night or not at all. A restaurant is chosen, a time agreed.

On Friday, Claudia eyes the *zabuton* in the center of the room. She fills the day in meditation, searching the darkness for something, anything, that will give her hope.

There is no money for a cab across town. Borrowing from Daphne is one thing, but she can't start hitting up neighbors, can she? Yet, what choice does she have? If Daphne doesn't lend her the money, which now seems likely, Claudia won't be able to repay even a small loan any time soon, and she wonders who in the building would be least affected. She knocks on the door of the peculiar lawyer who lives across the hall and never speaks to the other residents. There is no answer. She tries the gay men in the very next apartment. Their pug dog barks from inside, but no one comes to the door. She knocks on Mr. Zhang's door and hears shuffling inside, a mumbled response, and footsteps. The door opens and it is not Mr. Zhang, but his father, recently arrived from China. He doesn't speak much English, and Claudia doesn't begin to know how to explain to the elder Mr. Zhang what she needs. She apologizes for disturbing him.

She does have just enough for the Metro, but would then not have a way to return after dinner, so unless she can beg a little cash from her sister, in addition to the check that may or may not be forthcoming, she will need that money to get home. And so she walks the 16 blocks to the restaurant Daphne has chosen, Asia Nora, at 22nd and M.

Although she leaves the condo more than an hour before the appointed time, she is fifteen minutes late. Blisters have formed on both feet and perspiration drips under her arms;

her hair is wind-blown, and she's certain she looks like the homeless person she is at risk of becoming.

She is shown to Daphne's table. Her sister is elegant in a lavender blouse, over-sized pearls, her hair blonder than Claudia remembers, but even in the candle-lit dimness she can see the impatient scowl on Daphne's face. Crossing the room, Claudia dodges waitresses and busboys, wishing the evening were over, that somehow she could fast-forward to its conclusion and whatever misery awaits her, as long she could endure it at home, alone. Daphne rises and embraces her stiffly. The women sit and immediately a server pours a glass of chardonnay from the bottle that waits on ice. Daphne, who already has a glass, raises hers toward Claudia in a wordless toast, and drinks. Claudia returns hers to the table untasted, although she can smell its buttery sweetness, and recognizes the famous Napa Valley label, a wine she could never afford even under the best of circumstances.

The waitress comes for their orders.

"I'm not hungry," Claudia says, although she hasn't eaten more than popcorn in days.

"Don't be ridiculous," Daphne says, and orders for both of them: a salad of arugula and beets with a ginger-mustard vinaigrette, pepper-crusted blackfin tuna steaks, rare, with pomegranate chutney, Nora's special brown fried rice, asparagus in plum sauce. The thought of so much rich food makes Claudia ill and for a moment she closes her eyes, looks for the light, feels only waves wash over her. She can't breathe.

"Are you all right?"

Claudia opens her eyes. Daphne leans back in her chair, as if to see her big sister better, to take her all in.

"Shouldn't I be?"

"You're so thin."

"You're looking well," Claudia says.

"Heard from your bastard husband?"

"Timothy's had some bad luck."

"I'm sure his lack of character had nothing to do with it."

Their salads come and Claudia picks at the wedges of grapefruit that crown the odd concoction. Talk shifts to Daphne. She loathes conferences like the one that has brought her to town. She's become one of the top sellers in her agency. She's dating an actor, nothing serious, and, no, Claudia wouldn't know who he is. The fish comes but when Claudia cuts through the black crust to the blood-red flesh, awash in the gaudy chutney, she feels as though she has sliced into her own stomach and she can't eat. She pretends to taste the rice, the asparagus. They order dessert.

"So how's that job?" Daphne asks. "I imagine that was a relief. I know you'll want to pay off the loan but there's no hurry. We can work out a plan. I'll send you a promissory note."

It never occurred to Claudia that Daphne would want to formalize the loan. Will there be interest? A mortgage? "Sure," she says. "Good idea. I do appreciate it."

The dessert comes: an unappetizing lump of passion fruit sorbet.

"The thing is," Claudia says, "I think I mentioned there's some lag time before the first paycheck." It would be just like Daphne to make her ask twice.

"Yes. So you said in your note. And that's why I wanted to talk to you, Claude. You've been hugely irresponsible, you know." She dips into the sorbet.

What little Claudia has eaten roils. This is the price she must pay, but she isn't sure she can.

"Really, your whole life. You've never saved a dime. Remember that job you had in high school waiting tables? You spent all that on clothes, as I recall, probably that hasn't changed from the look of your new outfit. You and Timothy traveled all over like you didn't have a care, Japan or wherever. It adds up, you know, puts you in debt to your eyeballs, am I right? And then you expected Daddy to bail you out. Or Mom. And now me."

Claudia is afraid she will throw up at the table. How's that for payback?

"You're my sister and I love you, but what am I supposed to do? Do I just keep sending you money for the rest of our lives? How is that fair?"

"This is it, D, I promise. There's the job, and this is just temporary."

"You're not doing drugs again, are you?"

Claudia sees the head of the woman at the next table turn in their direction. She lowers her voice. "Again? What are you talking about?"

"You and that boy you dated."

"We were in college, for Christ's sake. We smoked pot."

"And got arrested, as I recall."

"A misunderstanding. And it's ancient history. I suppose you've never done anything you regret? No blemishes on your report card. Dad never came to the rescue?" No, Claudia realizes. Probably not. Daphne never did anything wrong, was always in control of her life, incapable of failure.

Daphne opens her wallet and pulls out a check she's already written. She puts it on the table and Claudia lets it sit there for a moment before she picks it up. But she does pick it up, as much as she would like to tell Daphne to go fuck herself.

"That's it, Claude. There won't be another one. This is the end."

She closes her eyes, imagines herself sitting in the center of her living room, and sees that point of light in the darkness where understanding resides but still eludes her. She has come from flesh, from parents who cared for her, who gave her a sister who has loved her in the only way she knows how, and yet she is as alone as anyone in this world can be. She is in the dark, in a confined space, under water, trying to breathe, waiting for her moment of light.

Her mother once told her that there would be times when

she felt as though she did not exist. That others around her—a husband, children, her children's children—would render her invisible. They would take their lives from her and she would have nothing left for herself.

But no one has taken her life. No one has effaced her, and that is the message of the point of light. She sees that now. That's the answer. It is her life, to do with as she pleases.

The check feels weightless in her hand.

THE NATIONS OF WITNESS

You may remember that the protagonist of my first novel is a corpulent salesman and sailing enthusiast who labors to build a seaworthy ketch as a way of coping with his beloved wife's insidious cancer and prolonged demise, but then is compelled to destroy the vessel—which he does with glorious pyrotechnics—when overwhelmed by grief. That the book garnered notice, and even a prize or two, was due in no small part, I believe, to the romantic strain of the age, one that demanded passion on a godly scale. The film version, in which the fire spreads to a tank of gasoline that ignites the entire marina, was, it seems to me, excessive, but cinema audiences, apparently, are not fond of subtlety, and so perhaps the conflagration was *de rigueur.* I suppose I should have taken that intemperance as a sign.

The success of my second book was not, I freely admit, a function of my scintillating prose. It was in all likelihood a hangover from the adulation heaped upon the first, together with the controversy attached to my inhabiting in those pages, for narrative purposes, the persona of a loathsome woman who leaves her writer-husband for the arms and bed of a younger female on whom she has long had her eye. That the scenario bore some resemblance to the tawdry conclusion of my first marriage struck some reviewers as writerly spite, better left to cocktail parties and the whispers of artists' communities and already-scandalous conferences in the Vermont mountains, but that very homomorphism sparked interest among both loyal and curious readers, and so the work blossomed into an international bestseller despite its evident flaws of sense and style. Even after the settlement of the inevitable lawsuit filed by my ex-wife and her partner, about which I am forbidden to speak owing to baroque covenants of confidentiality, the royalties garnered by that slim volume continue to underwrite my current lifestyle and, in particular, have relieved me of the excruciating burden borne by many of my less fortunate contemporaries of exposing semi-literate undergraduates to the neglected arts of readin' and writin'.

The novel in which I am currently engaged, entitled *The Nations of Witness*, I speak of now only reluctantly and at the behest of my publisher, who, as one might imagine, wishes to build pre-publication "buzz" for an endeavor the success of which is by no means assured. At least this time, in all candor, there should be little or no question as to the alter-identity of the protagonist, a man who in most respects—his age and demeanor, his sexual proclivities, his unbounded egoism—resembles the author. Whether the tale I tell is at all autobiographical I leave to readers and critics, but I will admit that my own life adventures have provided a wealth of material from which to draw.

The setting for the novel is tri-continental, as our lovable rogue-hero travels from his native Washington, D.C.—Current Seat of Global Domination, where he was reared in modest circumstances but managed to make a place for himself among the ruling elite, primarily by virtue of his own assiduity and innate intelligence—to the Capital City of the Future, Beijing, China, and thence to the twin Imperial Cities of the Past, London and Paris. Along the way, as replacement for an early love who meets an untimely and mysterious death (in a twist that allows me to avoid the tedium of recounting yet again the erstwhile spouse's latent lesbianism and ultimate betrayal), he acquires an exotic wife rumored to be descended from Qing emperors. After their lavish wedding amidst the ruins of a Tibetan monastery, the new wife discloses that she has borne and secreted among relatives exiled to France a daughter sired by a minor European monarch. And so the pair travel to Paris to reclaim the child, encountering on their journey numerous pecuniary and legal obstacles, those fire-breathing dragons of the modern quest, until the family is at last reunited in a humble, but historic, chateau on the outskirts of the City of Lights, where our hero sets about writing a novel about his travels, also called, in full metafictional circularity, *The Nations of Witness.*

But enough about the book.

My own odyssey has also been tri-continental, beginning not in Washington, D.C., but in the more sequestered Martha's Vineyard estate to which my father, the son of a noted industrial figure, was heir. From there my story shifts to St. Martin's, a prep school so exclusive that it barely registers on the collective psyche, then to Harvard, etc., all of which—including my family's precipitous decline thanks to the profligacy of my father's generation of alcoholic males and promiscuous females, not to mention various degenerate cousins, drug-addicted uncles and murderous aunts—is well documented. Fast forward through the first book and first marriage which, as young people say, seemed like a good idea at the time, to my inaugural trip to China. This was in that singular age when people didn't go to Old Cathay for either business, of which there was none but the most clandestine, or tourism, which was still outrageously uncomfortable and so tightly controlled as to be claustrophobic, or for any reason at all other than to say to their friends and family, "I've been to China," which, to be frank, was also my sole motivation. I would like to assert that I was conducting research for a book, particularly since I may well have made such a claim on a tax return of that era, but honesty precludes me. I was simply at loose ends (the marriage having recently imploded), had a bit of cash for the first time since I discovered my father had plundered my trust fund in order to finance his legal defense on a host of state and federal criminal charges (including tax evasion, fraud, and racketeering) and had, sadly, little or nothing with which to engage my soul.

It was on a visit to Nanjing that I met my second wife, who, at the time (this being after the monumentally tragic Cultural Revolution) was one of the intellectual lights of the emerging artistic community in that city. I was then even leaner than I am these days, tall by Asian standards, with a rugged if not quite handsome face but no trace of this gray beard. It was in all modesty no wonder to me that this lithe Chinese beauty should find me attractive. But beyond the physical, despite linguistic obstacles—her French was, for reasons that only became clear to me later, far superior to her rudimentary English, so that was the language in which we most often communicated—we found a connection such as I had never before felt, certainly not with my first wife, who, it should now be clear, withheld from me crucial information from the moment of our first meeting. Mei-ling showed me the sites in Nanjing, the empire's old Southern Capital: the city wall, the Confucian Temple, the underground art scene, the state-sanctioned and, even for those miserable times, sterile galleries. We dined simply in both nameless speakeasies, where my presence provoked hushed stares, and state-run canteens in which the air was filled with the acrid smoke of burning oil.

In the course of our exploration Mei-ling narrated for me Nanjing's historic calamity at the hands of the brutal Japanese invaders. Because I was until then ignorant of this aspect of local culture, the scale of the crime affected me profoundly. How could it have escaped my attention all those years? For reasons that I did not then fully comprehend, I felt the need to learn more like a rapacious thirst, and so I hungrily asked to meet survivors of the massacre. From them I heard firsthand accounts. What they revealed of the slaughter, its brazenness and brutality, only made me crave more.

This was the seed of the book that is only now nearing fruition, although I didn't realize its potential at the time. All I knew then was that these people were a link to history, corroborators of events I had not seen with my own eyes, a window to our shared past. In fact, I did not think of it as a book project until Mei-ling and I moved to Paris, where, coincidentally, we became acquainted with an elderly Jewish couple who had experienced the horrors of the Nazi occupation. It occurred to me then, and I only become more firmly convinced as the years go by, that in some ways the world is united by being witness to unspeakable evil. We seem to be powerless to prevent it from arising, and we do not succeed in stopping it (when we recognize it at all) even by flinging ourselves under its wheels. But what we can do, and have done unfailingly through millennia of malevolence, is give voice to the victims.

But I race ahead of myself, like a decoupled locomotive.

No doubt you are familiar with Mei-ling's work. She thought of herself as a sculptress, to use the sexist term that was common at the time, although her creations have always transcended mere sculpture. She builds communities of art, whole cities of work that interact and reflect the environment in which they arise. Today we might call her an installation artist, but I believe such a term trivializes what a successful environmental architect, to employ my own coinage, actually achieves. One of Mei-ling's designs, sadly never built, having been runner-up in a corrupted international competition, was a memorial to the victims of the Nanjing Massacre. It is true that the memorial would have cost a small fortune to execute, and covered a hectare or so of scarce arable land as it involved the forging of thousands of full-scale bronze corpses—adults, children, and even infants—to represent the hundreds of thousands who died in that atrocity. To me, though, once I learned the extent of the Japanese wickedness (that even during my time in school must have been airbrushed out of the history books), the labor and expense, the sheer immensity of the project, were clearly justified.

As a foreigner, it was difficult in those days for me to remain in China for long periods, and so I came and went. While I was in the country, according to a well-placed acquaintance, the secret police kept me under constant surveillance, which made my dalliance with Mei-ling both awkward and dangerous for her. What I did not know at the time, however, was that Mei-ling was already in disfavor with the Ministry of Culture and the local authorities for having traveled abroad previously and for having borne a child overseas who remained beyond the clutches of the totalitarian state and, therefore, unavailable as a tool with which to coerce Mei-ling's malleability. Which is not to say they could not make life difficult for her and her family. They did. There were frequent summonses to district and city police bureaus, unannounced searches of the family home, arbitrary closure of gallery shows and seizure of her drawings as "evidence" of her crimes. Eventually, though, perhaps weary of their own game, they allowed Mei-ling to leave the country, and we were reunited in Paris where we, as do the heroes of my new fiction, set about to liberate Xiao Mei, Little Plum, from the relatives who had been caring for her during the intervening years.

Little Plum, even at the age of seven when I first set eyes on her, had a regal bearing that turned heads. Indeed, as the novel-in-progress suggests, we believed her to have noble blood on both sides, from the Qing Dynasty on her mother's and the royal family of a once-thriving European principality on her father's, and the mix was like an exquisite hybrid orchid, conceivable only under the most extraordinary hothouse conditions. After wresting custody from the wicked stepmother, a grim woman straight from the pages of a dark fairy-tale who earned a pension from the monarch for raising the child, we took her with us wherever we traveled. With her fine Eurasian features, like a mysterious beauty in a Russian novel, it was painful to look away from her or, indeed, for her to be out of my sight for more than an instant.

Such intense longing led—somewhat to my surprise, although in retrospect understandably and predictably—to growing tensions between Little Plum's mother and me. Mei-ling suspected that my interest in the girl was more than paternal, complicated by the undeniable fact that we were no blood relation, and contrived to keep us apart by enrolling her in various boarding schools across Europe. As you might surmise, the separation achieved the opposite of its desired effect, and I found myself, with the handy excuse of conducting interviews among Holocaust survivors and their families, making frequent visits to the regions in which these schools were located. Eventually, although my love for Mei-ling and hers for me still burned bright, we found ourselves in constant battle over the child, and our union collapsed.

It was during this period that I came to Washington, at first because Mei-ling had placed Little Plum in a fine school in nearby Middleburg, and then, after her mother yanked her back to France, because I enjoyed the city's almost-European feel and the availability of documents and research institutions that were invaluable in my work on the current project which, by this time, had dragged on for nearly a decade. Little Plum was now a teenager and wrote to me regularly. She often occupied my thoughts, and not always in a way that a father should think of his daughter. But of course she was *not* my daughter, and so I began to rationalize these feelings while at the same time being consumed with the burden of guilt, the perpetual struggle with temptation. It occurred to me then that if Mei-ling and Little Plum were in France, it would be best for me to be elsewhere, at a great distance with an ocean between us, so that I might better battle this particular demon, and so I engaged a real estate agent to find a home in our nation's capital.

The Chinatown area appealed to me, for obvious reasons, although its Chinese-ness at this point is purely vestigial and increasingly artificial. This building in particular—my home and office, my refuge—struck me instantly as ideal for my purposes given its name: Nanking Mansion. What better place to write about the massacre than in a dwelling named (although long before the event, and with the old-style transliteration) for the decimated city in which the massacre occurred. I was also drawn to the space by the thriving arts community in the vicinity—lofts and studios and even a growing number of galleries abound, all pleasant reminders of my dear Mei-ling and, perhaps, an attraction for her should our relationship evolve such that we might consider reconciliation. The final selling point, the deal-maker as the agent might have said if I had revealed it to her, was my spotting two young boys, later known to me as Wesley and Simon Zhang, who in many respects—their hybrid facial features, the light skin, the less-than-black hair—reminded me of Little Plum. I knew immediately that they were the blessed children of Chinese and European parents, and if I could not be with Little Plum then I would delight in the presence of these charming boys.

And, for a time, the environment I built for myself was, to borrow a phrase from the installation work at which Mei-ling still excels, satisfying. The condominium suited me well, with fine light and ample space. It was not far from the Library of Congress and a short taxi ride to the Holocaust Museum, both important sources for my work. I did not see the Zhang boys as often as I thought I might, although I must have startled them with my beaming smiles whenever I did encounter them as they headed out for a stroll with their charming mother, who I understand has since passed on in a tragic automobile accident. The work progressed well, if slowly, but each time I saw the boys, or even their over-polite father, with whom I had occasion to exchange what few words of Chinese I possessed, I could not but think of Little Plum. Our correspondence continued and that sustained me, but in time I realized I needed more and conceived of a plan to be implemented on the occasion of her eighteenth birthday, which was then only a few months hence.

I would find a tenant for the Washington apartment, which was easily accomplished through the auspices of my realtor and acquaintances in the literary community. And I would secure a suitable flat in Paris to which I would relocate for the purpose of completing the new book, finally, and also, of course, being more readily available to Little Plum should she, having reached her majority, choose to seek me out.

Which, to Mei-ling's horror and my delight, she did. So, I admit to you, the rumors that have filtered through the literati and into the annals of popular scandal are true: my wife's teenage daughter became my lover. When Little Plum confirmed this state of affairs to her mother over the telephone, Mei-ling understandably dropped out of sight and contact with us both, after, that is, one last encounter.

There was a soft knock at our door that I knew must be hers, and there she was: eyes red and flooded, jaw set, as if girded for battle. Yet none came.

"You must be mad," she said. Her voice quavered. When Little Plum appeared behind me a faint gasp escaped Mei-ling's lips. "Both of you. Mad."

And then she vanished into the darkness like a moonstruck demon.

We heard of her from time to time after that through

friends, friends of friends, and saw occasional newspaper reports of her comings and goings, especially in the European editions of the American press, but we did not communicate. Even with the germ of guilt that we both felt, the inescapable notion that we had hurt a woman we still loved, Little Plum and I were blissfully happy in our Parisian life.

Our flat was mere steps from the Seine. While I wrote, she painted—with considerable skill, I pridefully noted—and began to show her work, mostly executed in watercolor but also gouache and oils, in up-and-coming galleries that favored only the most promising emerging painters and sculptors. Imagine: an exotic young beauty in Paris possessing talent beyond her years, mingling with an incomparably vibrant assemblage of artists from around the globe. It was perhaps inevitable that she would find suitors among the young men (and women!) who flocked to her bright light. We both mocked the females who thought they stood a chance, she because, I believed, that phase in her experimentation had already passed, and I, less confidently, because of the unhappy history of my first marriage. And, for the most part, we also laughed together over the proposals she received from men, those visitors who would call upon us at the flat at all hours of the day and night, visibly shocked when it was I and not Little Plum who responded to their persistent knocking at our door or their raucous serenading from the *allée* below our windows.

But a time came when one young painter stood out from among the rest, and the laughter ceased. I met him at the opening of a show of his work: brilliantly original portraits of winged men and horses amidst post-apocalyptic chaos and despair. I accompanied Little Plum, whom he called Mu-shu, as if she were a take-out carton of gelatinous pork, and saw how her normal self-assuredness receded with his approach, how she lowered her eyes when he looked at her, how the palms of her tiny hands, which I held in order to disabuse myself of the conclusion I was fast approaching, grew damp in his presence. He was a handsome boy, tall, broad-shouldered, with Middle-Eastern features—dark complexion and hair, slightly narrow-set eyes, elongated nose—that I could not at first place more precisely but that I later learned were Kurdish.

"Nathan Baxter," I said, offering my hand when Little Plum failed to make the introductions.

"Hadi," he said without affectation. "An honor to meet you, sir." His firm grip relaxed, and his attention and bright, welcoming smile turned to his Mu-shu.

How it pained me to see them together! And my discomfort was exacerbated by the boy's obvious talent, his gentleness, his deference toward me and his well-bred solicitousness toward my Little Plum. I quite liked him, in fact, and learned from Little Plum's tentative biography that his own family had experienced some of the horrors that I have been exploring all these years.

When I invited the young man to visit us at the flat, Little Plum looked at me as though I had in that instant sprouted horns and a barbed tail, but on the evening he did in fact appear she sat quietly, doe-eyed, while between us, he and I, we downed three bottles of a passable Burgundy, and they, he and she, smoked a joint the size of my index finger. It seemed to me that we both, she and I, were reluctant to see him leave that evening. As odd as it sounds, I felt as if I had found a match for my daughter—my daughter who was also my lover. Although it took some doing to convince her that I was at peace with the outcome, we both knew that our improbable affair had reached its end. When next we saw the young man, I embraced them both and left, to stroll along the Seine, to be alone with my thoughts.

And I naturally thought of my apartment in Washington, since Paris could no longer be home for me.

Artists are generally not practical people, but I have always prided myself on possessing enough sense to get by, and then some. However, in leaving Paris precipitously I apparently gave no consideration to the fact that I had previously leased my condominium to a pleasant young couple, even though I had until recently been receiving regular reports from my realtor indicating that the rent (a modest sum because the couple was somehow related to an acquaintance and in a moment of weakness I'd agreed to below-market rates) had been paid and was accumulating in the bank account we had established for that purpose. It seems I also failed to recall that in the prior two months I had instead of these reports received complaints from said realtor that the rent, out of which she deducted her commission, had failed to arrive. And yet, despite the information that should have been at my disposal, upon arrival at Dulles International Airport I taxied to my marginal neighborhood, climbed the few steps up to the building's charmless entrance with a suit-bag slung over my shoulder, stepped into the long, wide hallway filled with the abstracts and collages of my fellow artist-residents, put the key in the lock of my unit, and pushed the door open.

Whereupon I nearly caused the very pregnant young woman who stood at the kitchen sink doing dishes to deliver her infant prematurely, although, judging from the size of her and the dropped position of the child in her womb, not by much. She was, of course, my tenant: half of the couple to whom I had rented the apartment many months earlier, and about whom I had until that moment utterly forgotten. I looked about for the husband or boyfriend, who I now remembered was a sturdy brute, but she was quite alone. As I backed out of the apartment with apologies for arriving unannounced, the young woman—having, I suppose, recognized me and regained her composure—beckoned me in with a wave of the dishtowel she still held in her delicate hand.

It must seem odd for me to have thought this when I had only of late been wholly enamored of my Little Plum, but I was as much startled by this girl's radiance as I was by her unexpected presence in my home. She, too, like Little Plum and the Zhang boys, was certainly of mixed race. In her case I detected American Indian and realized even as I lingered in the doorway that my thinking about genocidal witness was incomplete: standing before me was a surviving descendant of one of European civilization's most thorough efforts at ethnic eradication.

She confirmed as much when I asked. In her family tree, she'd been told, were a number of Monacans, a branch of the Cherokee that inhabited the southern Appalachians, and that explained the early-dusk complexion, the black straw hair, the almond eyes. I had more questions, which she surely thought peculiar, and sat at her kitchen table—my kitchen table, I realized, as I had rented the place to the couple furnished—drinking tea and listening to her patient answers.

"I should be going," I finally said, no longer able to ignore the lateness of the hour. I placed my hands on the table as if to rise, but did not do so.

"Don't," she said. "I mean, you don't have to."

And so it happened that the girl, Susanna, invited me to stay on the living room couch (my study being used by her for her canvases and paints, for she, too, was a budding artist). I protested, naturally, but I admit that I was pleased by the offer, not only because I did not relish spending the night in a hotel, but also because I longed to be near the young mother-to-be.

I became, then, a houseguest in my own home: too charmed, too enraptured by her state to evict my rent-delinquent tenant and take my rightful place. She worked, I soon learned, in a coffee shop, which allowed me unfettered hours during the day to compose, using the dining room table, hand writing on yellow tablets. The conditions brought back fond memories of the early days, toiling on the first novel, inventing the world beyond my own kitchen. Susanna would return in the evenings and we would talk about the many characters who flowed through her shop: the homeless men who were permitted use of the restroom by the benevolent manager; the arrogant young professionals who drudged in nearby office blocks; the artists and writers from the surrounding community, momentarily emerging from their studios and apartments to partake of the world before re-immersing themselves in the artificial environments of their own creation, most of them without ever noticing the real thing. We would dine together simply, on hearty soups that I concocted, having acquired passable cooking skills from both of my ex-wives (for by this time Mei-ling had arranged to dissolve our union, a sad inevitability), and fresh bread Susanna brought home from a bakery she passed en route.

In complete candor, I was grateful for her condition, which, though it aroused in me a robustly prurient fantasy, established a barrier between us that prevented me from acting on my viler instincts. With each hour the arrangement grew more natural, Susanna more trusting, I more hopeful.

Suspicious of my intentions, the other residents of Nanking Mansion maintained a certain wariness for which I could scarcely blame them.

I had been in the apartment for only a day when we had our first visitors. The Zhang boys knocked on the door and Susanna admitted them along with a cat, a brindled creature that was not, I was given to understand by my tenant, technically permitted either by the lease she and her erstwhile boyfriend had signed with me or by the rules of the building's Homeowners Association (she had made discreet inquiries when she first noticed the cat hovering near the back alley trashcans). The boys eyed me cautiously, perhaps remembering our first meeting during my brief residency in the building when their mother was still alive, and I, of course, thought only of Little Plum: I saw her in their hazel eyes, their skin, their hair. The cat, too, was intrigued and wound through and around my legs as if investigating not only my identity but pedigree and feline compatibility. The boys departed, leaving the cat, but a few moments later there was another knock on the door.

Mr. Zhang, their father, stood in the doorway bearing a plate of oranges.

"For Miss Susanna," he said, stepping into the apartment at Susanna's invitation, accompanied by the bracing scent of citrus. He studied me with no less curiosity than had the cat before him. He glanced around the living room. He looked at Susanna, who then was busying herself at the stove boiling water for tea, and then back to me.

I nodded. Should I have justified myself to this man who was so clearly there to investigate what his sons had just reported? Had I done something that required explanation? Did I not have a right to be present in my own home?

He left, apparently satisfied, and Susanna explained that Mr. Zhang and his elderly father had been most helpful to her after Thomas moved out, the circumstances of his departure being left so ambiguous that I found it difficult to refrain from inquiring further about the father of this girl's child. In any case, before I could explore the matter, there was yet another knock on the door.

Now the portly Armenian, Sam Artoyen, the building's developer and manager, filled the doorway, presenting me with yet another descendent of the world's martyred races. I made mental notes as to the gaps in my research, resolved to question the man even as he made his excuses for having intruded. No sooner had the door closed behind him than there was another knock.

This time it was a young African American man who greeted Susanna with a not-altogether dispassionate kiss. Momentarily I wondered if this man might not be the Thomas of whom Susanna had spoken, the father of the child and, I'd thought, the ex-boyfriend. But, no: I'd met Thomas once upon a time when the lease was signed. This gentleman, upon introduction, was Aloysius, another helpful neighbor who, it was soon evident, knew his way around Susanna's, which is to say *my*, apartment, as if it were his own.

We three sat at the table and sipped tea, and it became clear that his perusal of me was to be more than the cursory examinations that had preceded it. I was interrogated—Aloysius was an attorney—and, I believe, was judged, if not benign, at least not immediately threatening. This questioning was an unsettling comfort, revealing as it did that the child-woman lived among those who cared so much for her that they would take it upon themselves to vet a new acquaintance in this manner. Were they justified in their concern? Were they right not to intervene? Did they, having perceived a danger to one of their tribe, somehow fail her? But what, exactly, should they have done?

It was not long after this—having realized as all our neighbors already had that our cohabitation was, if not inappropriate, unseemly—that I broached a delicate subject with Susanna. She was living, after all, rent-free in my apartment, and, while I thoroughly enjoyed her company, our arrangement was one that could not continue: we needed to explore alternatives before the baby came.

"Susanna, my dear," I began. "Have you considered where you will go?" I only meant that surely she had made plans, that she knew the rent had not been paid in some months, that she could not stay with me indefinitely, and that it would be best for all concerned to complete whatever long-term-arrangements were necessary before the baby's arrival complicated matters further.

"Go?" she asked.

At which point Susanna clutched her belly and shrieked as if I had kicked her. She crumpled upon herself and looked at me, wordlessly pleading with me to make the agony stop, except that by the time she reached the floor the excruciating moment had passed. As she sat there, leaning against the kitchen cabinets, breathing heavily, a stunned alertness filled her eyes. There was pounding on the door, shouts of "Susanna" in the hallway that I recognized as the voice of Aloysius, and I hurried, grateful for his arrival, to let him in. He looked menacingly at me and then, perhaps sensing that I was not the cause of Susanna's cry, rushed to her side.

We telephoned for help, but there was no time. Instructions from Susanna's obstetrician were relayed by telephone through me, and Aloysius followed them meticulously with my assistance where needed. If this truly was the girl's first child, as the speed of its delivery caused me to suspect it was not, the arrival of her squalling baby boy even before the paramedics arrived was one for the record books. And I was there to see the signal event, Susanna's suffering, the frightening spill of serous fluid across my floor, the bloody head as it thrust its way into my world.

While she was in the hospital with the child, whom she named Loyal, after her father, I conceived of a scheme that was at once both outlandish and sublime. The sight of the piteous infant had moved me beyond reason. I was in a position to change the course of history, not just to stand idly by while mother and son vanished from sight and memory, but to preserve them. I would marry Susanna and adopt Loyal. We would live in the condo. I would finish the book that would shift from its dark underpinnings of atrocity to a more hopeful conclusion about the power of witness, how it takes visions of horror for mankind to appreciate the miracle of rebirth. I would relegate Mei-ling to my past, along with Little Plum, and my future would be with this new, accidental family. Each day while she was gone I walked, seeing the neighborhood as I'd never experienced it before, the city as a new life with limitless potential.

On the day Susanna was to come home, I spent the morning at the Library of Congress. The good Aloysius, as planned, was to pick her up and bring mother and child back to Nanking Mansion in the late afternoon, and so I meandered from Capitol Hill to our building, turning corners and circling blocks to make the time pass, in order to consider what I might say to her, how I could propose this change in our relationship in a way that might persuasively convey the benefits it promised for all. Each attempt I abandoned as inadequate, and by the time I entered the apartment, my limbs burning with exhaustion, I had no better idea what I should say than when I began.

Although I had visited tiny Loyal in the hospital, I was anxious to see him in his new home, where he might thrive until we could find something larger, with room for him to grow. Perhaps room for another child. But there was no Loyal in residence. No Susanna. The furniture was all mine and so that remained in place, but Susanna's few possessions—the easel and paints, the canvases and brushes, the clothes from her closet and the stuffed animals from her bed, even her hodgepodge of dishes and glassware—were gone, as if she had never been there at all, as if she had been the product of a novelist's over-fertile imagination.

But she *had* been there. I had seen her. I had heard her scream. I had felt her death grip on my arm and smelled her fear and blood. I had watched her writhe in agony and give birth on the floor of my blessed kitchen.

As I thought about it, I knew where they were.

And soon, not today or tomorrow, but in a few days, I will walk down the hall and knock on their door. I will say nothing of what I had planned. I will play my part as the kind, solicitous neighbor, asking after the baby. I will bring a gift, perhaps, something for Loyal, a bauble for Susanna. I will shake Aloysius's hand heartily and will wish him well, congratulate him for coming to Susanna's aid, for standing between her and tragic fate. And I will continue to work on my book, which will no doubt revert to its darker tone. I will conclude in those pages, as you may already have guessed, that we are all witness to the atrocities of history, that it is our obligation to speak out for those who cannot, those victims who bear the burden of evil for us all. But, though we raise our voices, though we protest, there is nothing we can do to prevent history from repeating itself. Again and again and again.

ARTOYEN'S RAZOR

Graceful as a three-hundred-pound rodent, I thump down to the basement of Nanking Mansion in hopes I won't be seen—a firm grip on the banister, wet towel draped over my arm, dopp kit tottering on my open palm—and nearly swallow my gold fillings when I spot the Chinese kid from Number 5 standing in the open doorway of the storeroom. There's my thrift-store mattress on the floor, the half-empty bottle of distilled sleep-aid in easy reach, and my secret's out.

"Mr. Artoyen," says the kid.

"Wesley," I say, guessing, not remembering which of the brothers this might be.

His sneakers squeak on the cement floor as he takes a backward step. "I'm Simon," he says. "How come you live in the closet?"

Words to live by: Never offer more than the customer wants, even if it's less than he needs. I don't particularly want the residents of the building to know I've been kicked out of my place in the 'burbs, and I sure as hell don't want my Shelley to find out. Or the buyers who are due here any minute. But the kid didn't ask the right question.

"I don't," I lie. "That's just for . . . naps."

The boy peers inside. Reminds me of me as a rug-rat back in Philly, snooping around the building where my dad was the super, sticking my nose where it didn't belong no matter how often he paddled my butt and told me to mind my own business. My shabby suitcase lies open next to the mattress, a jumble of boxer shorts and socks. I drop the towel and kit inside and pull the door shut.

"Look, Wesley—"

"Simon."

"—Simon," I say, "let's make this our little secret." Kids keep secrets all the time. It's like a law of nature. With the right incentive, my lips were always sealed tighter than a priest's. I pull a dollar from my wallet and hand it to the kid. "Just between us."

He clutches the bill and runs up the stairs in a squeaky barrage. Will he tell his father? Not if he understands the value of a buck. That's what's great about this country. A deal is sacred. Offer, acceptance, done. He'll tell his little brother, sure, but they're just kids. Didn't I share everything with Raffi when we were that age? And besides, the storeroom is temporary, my run of bum luck about to end. Guaranteed. Sixty minutes from now, when the last condo sells, I'll be out from under. Free of my ex. Breathing room.

Kemal pulled the rented Jetta to the curb mid-block. They were early to meet the owner, this Artoyen character, not a bad thing. They might catch him off guard, learn a little something they wouldn't otherwise. He studied Bettina's face to gauge her reaction to the neighborhood, about which he was skeptical himself. Was it on the way up? Or down? But had she seen it the same way? He could always tell what his wife was thinking. Her pouty lips, the crinkled nose, those dancing eyebrows—they said it all. She'd be a tough sell.

Bettina leaned forward to look at the building through the windshield. Hadn't Kemal mentioned Georgetown?

She'd heard of Georgetown, with the tony shops and stately townhomes. But they'd just driven under a gaudy Chinese arch and past a crumbling row of boarded-up shanties. This definitely wasn't Georgetown.

I hustle the young couple by the two artists loitering in the hallway—the angry sculptor and the moody painter—and into the condo they've come to see, Number 7, the only one left. I nod and wave, have to make nice, but do I stop and chat? No, I do not. Those artistic types are a selling point, sure. Everyone thinks they're going to want to hang around with the artists. Culture and that crap. But look close and it's a different story.

That tall one? Always a cigarette in his face, a goddamn volcano. Take a tip from Sam Artoyen, big-time Washington D.C. real-estate developer from the mean streets of Philadelphia P-A, those things will cook your lungs, have you crazy for air by the time you're fifty, even if you quit, which isn't exactly cake. And if you don't, like my old man, pretty soon you're tied to an oxygen tank for the rest of your sorry life. On top of that, the kid screws anything that moves, always a new girl leaving his place. I watch my building. I see things. Keep your wives and daughters away from that one! If my Sammy grows up like that, I'll shoot myself. If I live so long.

Then there's the other one, the little guy, smelling of paint and booze, eyes glazed over. Not just high on life, I'll wager. Red hair frizzed like a clown. Is that the sort of man a young couple wants for a neighbor? Not if they're thinking of children they don't. Scar the kids for life.

I clear my throat and the gurgle echoes in the empty apartment.

"This unit is particularly spacious," I say in my smarmiest real-estate voice. It's the smallest apartment in Nanking Mansion, but do they need to know? I bought this run-down building cheap, deep leverage. Throw out the tenants, gut the place, knock down a few walls, toss in a skylight or two, then don my salesman hat, turn on the charm, make a tidy profit. If I can get them all sold, which hasn't been easy.

"You love the open floor plan. Am I right?"

The girl nods and smiles, like some dashboard bobblehead. The guy marches into the place as if he's lived there for years. Waits for nothing. No manners, this one.

I shut the door behind us, open a window for air, hope they don't notice the musty smell, and start the tour in the kitchen. I give a friendly pat to the appliances I picked out myself, middle-grade Kenmores. Not fancy, but the young lady will love them.

"You've got your professional cooking surface here," I say, although I say that about every stove in every unit. "You love to cook. Am I right?"

The girl giggles, the guy snorts like the pig he is, and I feel sweat trickling under my arms.

Kemal liked the spacious apartment on the edge of Chinatown, and getting to work on the Metro would be a snap, but something about Sam Artoyen didn't seem right. He claimed he was the developer, or contractor, or sales agent for this ex-tenement (the story changed each time he told it). But it was Artoyen's hair Kemal didn't trust, the toupee that wasn't fooling anyone. The guy wheezed. He was built like a hot-air balloon. And he stank. Was that licorice?

Bettina thought the condo was too modern, with all its blond wood and bright colors: sea-foam green in the kitchen, goldenrod in the bedroom. She'd had something more traditional in mind, like her mother's place. Plus, she worried about Mr. Artoyen's weight, the folds of fat spilling over the waist of his stylish suit pants, jiggling beneath the silk shirt. But Bettina hoped to find work in a gallery and Mr. Artoyen—Sam, he insisted—Sam promised to help, said he was something of an artist himself and connected in the art world.

Kemal suppressed a smile when the guy said that; it was just the kind of line he'd use himself. A man after Kemal's own heart.

Truth is, I don't want to sell this place. I've got no choice. This building, the Nanking Mansion, was going to be my crowning achievement, if that's not too grand a phrase for a lump of real estate. Look at it! Think of what it was before! I did this, something to be proud of, fixed up an eyesore, helped turn this city around. After fifty long years of getting by, cutting corners, nose to the grindstone, I was going to kick back, and Shelley and I, if she would have me, a fat impostor twice her age, would move in, have a kid, wait for the neighborhood to blossom, make a killing, move to Palm Springs, live the good life. But the whole picture's changed now. Another of life's rules: Nothing's ever as good as it seems. The ex-wife is nagging me for money, says I owe it to her. My boy needs braces, says I should pay for college. What's more, the doctors tell me I could go at any minute. A fucking time bomb. So what's the point?

And what's with this kid, Kemal, last name Tuzmen. A Turk is he? The things my grandfather told me about Istanbul gave me nightmares as a kid. Should I do business with a murderous Turk?

"And that view!" I say to the girl. "It's not much right now, but my sources tell me the city plans to turn that vacant lot into a park. Trees, flowers, the works!" Sources! It could happen.

The first thing Kemal noticed as they toured the outside of the building was the rubble in the alley: a heap of bricks and dirt, not to mention the swirling newspapers, beer cans tumbling in the wind, and was that a hypodermic needle?

When he gazed skyward, his doubts escalated. On the third floor a flapping sheet of plastic half-covered a hole in the wall. He looked for Artoyen to get an explanation, but the fat man had turned Bettina's attention, with his grubby hand on her elbow, toward the pipe-dream urban park he'd conjured. Not likely, in this neighborhood. Still. The condo was a steal, and it was the only place they'd seen in the city that worked for them financially. Unless Bettina's mom kicked in for a down-payment, which wasn't going to happen. So what if the old Armenian was a crook? Two could play that game, just got to keep the eyes open.

What Bettina noticed was that Sam had missed a spot shaving, that the lower half of his right cheek was covered in gray stubble. His shoes were dull, too, scuffed, as if hidden by clouds, not the sunny shine of Kemal's Florsheims.

They're an unlikely couple. Like me and my ex. Connie worked in an office, said she needed stability. But I'm not like that, never could be. No wonder it didn't last between us. What did this kid say he did? Something about a non-profit company. What's the point of that? Do they make money or don't they? And her? Wants to work in a gallery, she says, likes working with artists. Is she nuts? Wait till she tries to collect from an artist! Wait till the first check bounces! I've had a hell of a time with so-called artists flaking out on contracts, missing deadlines, even stealing paintings right off the wall. If this place depended on artists it wouldn't exist. Take our private "Gallery" in the long entrance hallway. They think I should pay them to let them hang their lousy pictures on my walls. It's clutter, if you ask me, these pictures of nothing anybody can recognize. They should pay me!

But they're not the worst. The black guy in Number 6 must be crazy to sledgehammer a hole in the wall like that. I don't care if he is a lawyer, I'm going to sue the bastard if he costs me this sale. I saw the Turk staring up at the plastic flying in the wind. What was I going to tell him? That his future neighbor is a goddamn crazy man?

"I have the paperwork right here," I say. I slap my briefcase to let them know I mean it. Then I look at my watch. "Got another showing in an hour." The act never gets old.

"Come on, babe," he says. Just a trace of whine. "Let's do it."

"I don't know," she says. It's more than just the condo she's having doubts about. I know the signs. My ex used to get that look in her eyes.

"Christ," says the guy.

Slowly, slowly. Push, but not too hard. Never let them see how desperate you are. "I'm expecting another offer," I say, but gently, without menace.

"Shouldn't we look around some more? Before we sign?"

"Christ," says the guy again.

"By all means, young lady. By all means." And so it goes.

Kemal was as uncertain about the neighborhood as Bettina, but she didn't need to know that. They both liked the idea of urban pioneering. After all, in Chicago they lived in a funky Andersonville two-flat, not exactly an isolated luxury high-rise on Lake Shore Drive or a colonial four-square in Winnetka. This area, though, looked like it had a long way to go before it emerged from whatever decline it had been in. Good investment potential, nowhere to go but up, but how long would he have to wait?

Bettina worried about safety, although she'd never admit it to Kemal, envisioning, if all went well, a baby in the not-too-distant future. A dark little guy like his papa, or maybe a blond like her. Or one of each! Would she be comfortable pushing a stroller down a street where refurbished Victorians rubbed shoulders with burned-out brownstones and crackhouses? The condo building, at least, seemed like a self-contained oasis. Without having met any of the neighbors, she dreamed of knocking on doors, dropping by for coffee, hosting dinner parties, building friendships that would last a lifetime. Was that baking bread she smelled?

Now we're back in the "Gallery," but at least those crazy artists are gone. The girl studies the ridiculous paintings on the wall as we pass, the guy doesn't see them, has a cell phone out to check messages.

"There's just communal storage downstairs, plus a shared exit to the alley," I say. Haven't they seen enough? But I open the fire-door to the steps and down they go. All these stairs, up, down. I lag behind. I'm beat.

"Well, hello," I hear the girl say. When I round the corner and catch up, I see why.

Simon peers up at me, the younger brother, Wesley, by his side. The lighting's not good but in the yellow fluorescence it looks as if they're both trembling. Wes has his hands behind him.

"What you got there, Wesley?" I ask. The older one doesn't correct me so I figure I got the name right. Pipsqueak steps behind his brother. I scare kids, it seems. Is that what happened with my Sammy?

"We found something," Simon says. Spokesboy, apparently. He whispers in Wesley's ear and the little one holds out his hand. My razor.

"We didn't tell," says Simon. "Honest."

I must have dropped the razor when Simon surprised me earlier. Since I've been living in the storeroom, I use the bathroom in the condo, up and down these back stairs, try to hide my tracks, and I'm always in a rush. It's not like I'm not entitled, of course. Technically, it's my place. I can use it if I want. Who's to say I can't? I snatch my razor out of the boy's hand—I don't mean to be rough but it must look that way—and the two of them run out the door into the alley.

The girl glares at me like I owe her an explanation. I shrug.

◆ ◆ ◆

Kemal wanted the kids to stick around, figured that's just what Bettina needed to push her over the edge. So when the Armenian chased them off, all Kemal could do was shake his head. For a guy who seemed pretty desperate to make a sale, that was exactly the wrong move.

Bettina was thrilled to see the boys, dark like Kemal, and wanted to talk to them. Why did Mr. Artoyen yell at them?

I don't know how much longer I can keep this up. It's all I can do to climb the stairs some days, and the huffing and puffing when I get there makes me feel like an old man. Doctor says it's a hole in my heart, cardio-my-something-or-other, says he can fix it, maybe. Worth a shot, he says. Easy for him. And these kids. Do they want to buy, or not? They're coming to town, he's dragging her kicking and screaming, they've got to live somewhere, there's no getting around that. Why not here? Let's make a deal!

They can't see what a goldmine this is. I did everything on the cheap, paid the right guys, cut the right corners. They move in, make a baby, buy a house in Silver Spring and sell this place for a nice profit before the appliances go bad, before the homeowners' association makes an assessment to replace the substandard roof, the HVAC system that's too small for a unit this size. A goldmine. Buy now!

We've seen the public areas downstairs and now we're back in the apartment. "You folks take a good look around," I say. "I'll be right here." I pull the papers out of the briefcase, arrange them on the counter, nice and neat, lay the pen next to the contract with the nib pointed toward the signature line, like the old man taught me. Of course that was TV sets and stereos, La-Z-boys and bedroom suites, but it's the same principle: show 'em where to sign, make it easy, works like a charm.

◆ ◆ ◆

The man was a good salesman, Kemal had to give him that. An impressive performance. He'd had enough experience in business to see through the snake oil, but he needed all the help he could get with Bettina. With Bettina and her mother, in truth, who was against the move, said he wasn't considering Bettina's career, Bettina's life. Her mother's life, more like. Getting Bettina away from that witch would be the best thing that ever happened to them. By all means, load those selling points and fire when ready. Museums a short walk away! Convention center! Arena! Shops, restaurants, parks! Bull's-eye! Artoyen even made up some great-schools crap, as if the guy had a clue about schools in the neighborhood, or whether children were even a consideration. Not any time soon, that was certain. But go ahead, tell her how great the schools are!

Bettina was pleased to hear about the schools, because that's exactly what she wanted to know but was afraid to ask in front of Kemal. Kids were something they fought about all the time, something her mother told her to keep pushing. But Mr. Artoyen said the right thing, and she stole a glance at Kemal rolling his eyes. She wondered if she might be able to come back on her own to take a look at that nice school.

Schools. What do I know from schools? I'm closer to the grave than I am to books and pencils. I see this girl's mind working. She's all about having babies, but her man wants no part of it. I give them a year or two, three tops, and then this place will be back on the market. Maybe, if I survive the heart thing, that surgery the doc wants to do, I can take it off their hands cheap, make the divorce easy for them. We all win.

And will Shelley have me when I tell her about the operation? Does it make sense for *us* to have the baby she wants, if I'm not going to be around? The whole thing makes me dizzy. Already got one teenager who won't give me the time of day, an ex-wife who's suddenly into yoga and making peace with her enemies, of which I guess I'm one. Or *the* one. Peace. How about cutting me some slack on the alimony? Do I really want more of this bullshit?

Kemal was itching to sign. He'd been pre-approved for the mortgage, the bank was still open, and he could be back in an hour with a cashier's check for the deposit. They'd been floundering in Chicago; it was time to get out of the clutches of Bettina's mother. She'd never approved of him, had even tried to talk Bettina out of getting married. With him standing right there, as if he didn't exist! Things would be different now. That woman wouldn't dictate to them another day.

Bettina clutched her cell phone and wanted to call her mother, to tell her they were about to make an offer on the condo. From a dozen previous calls, though, she knew what her mother would say: Kemal didn't treat her right, didn't consider what she wanted, he'd be a lousy father, too many women in his past, how could she be sure there were none in the present? Kemal said it seemed she was married to her mother instead of him. Ridiculous, said Mother, wake up before it's too late. She paced around the bedroom, keeping clear of Kemal. In the master bath the floor was damp. A bar of soap glistened in the tub.

I head upstairs to see what's taking so long, every step a struggle, and I'm breathing hard when I get there. But I can see they're ready, or at least the guy is, from the way he seems to be bowing toward his wife, pleading. This, what's her name, Betty, is a nice girl, but she's got no idea what she's getting into. That's obvious. She has no chance against him, not when he pulls the old begging stunt. We're in this together, Kemal and me, and I do my part. I close the blinds so she won't see the alley down below, that hoodlum kid Eddie and his drug-dealing brother. Speaking of kids, I should get those Chinese kids back in here, be nice, make up for before. That's the card to play now. Let Betty get a good look and she'll be ready to buy in a heartbeat. Speaking of heartbeats, I should have put a chair in the place. Out of breath. Need to sit down.

Just what Kemal needed. Artoyen wasn't looking too good, turned pale all of a sudden, at the moment he nearly had Bettina convinced. Trying to buy a house and the agent practically croaks on them. Down the stairs he went, breathing as loud as a freight train, left them alone up in the bedroom while he sat at the bottom of the steps. Now was Kemal's chance to seal the deal with Bettina, before it was too late, before Artoyen could blow it. What do you think, hon?

When Sam closed the blinds, Bettina grew curious about what they could see from the apartment, and the answer was not much. She opened the window and saw a couple of kids up to no good, empty beer cans and yellowed newspaper in the alley. There was an abandoned warehouse right behind them, and that couldn't be good, either, a magnet for trouble. Was Sam telling the truth about his connections with galleries? Or the planned park? The school? Anything? She had a perfectly good job in Chicago, so why were they moving? Because Kemal wanted to move. Mother was right.

Now that my breathing is steady, I can hear again: they're too quiet. Are they whispering, or what? I hear footsteps on the laminate, the girl, crossing the room and opening the window, so she sees reality that way. That's for the best, I suppose. It is what it is. Had to happen eventually. A cell phone rings. Finally I can hear her voice and it's getting louder. An instant later they're on the steps coming down. I boost myself to my feet and she's past me and already heading through the Gallery and back out to the street. What the hell happened?

◆ ◆ ◆

What the fuck happened? Bettina's mother, that's what. One minute Kemal was close to making an offer on the condo and the next she's yakking on the phone with the old bag and glaring at him like he kicked her puppy.

What on earth happened? Why was Bettina even considering this move? Kemal didn't ask her, he just announced, "We're moving." Mother finally made her see. He didn't know she had options. There was a vacant apartment in Mother's building; it would only take one call, she said. One call.

Never accept as true that which could be a profitable lie. That's my number one motto. Think about it. The girl storming out like that. It's a scam, right? Think the price will come down? I'm not falling for tricks. And anyway, I'm not sorry to see them go. You know why? Life's short. I'm going to go down to Shelley's place right now and propose. I'll say, I know I'm a fat old man with a weak ticker, but you and I are meant to be together. And then I'll bring her over here, and sell her on this place just like I was selling these kids. Only her I'll tell the truth, mostly, that it's a temporary thing, and by the time our kid, if we have a kid, is ready for school, we'll be long gone. And I'll tell her it's safe enough, as safe as anywhere else in this town. And I'll tell her I'm going to lose weight and I'll have that operation and I'll be good as new. I'll find the money to pay Connie, even if I have to get a regular job. I'll patch things up with Sammy, turn into a real dad. We'll all have a nice long life together. Starting now.

"Bettina, honey, wait," Kemal said. "I didn't mean all that about your mother. It's just that this is the right move for us. A way to be out on our own." He tried a different tack: "The apartment's big and your mother can visit any time." And another: "There's even room for a nursery!"

Bettina did like the idea of being a little more independent from her mother, who could at times be controlling. And she'd known Kemal would eventually come around on having a baby. He mentioned the nursery! That was all she needed to hear.

I need to start my life over. But first I need to lie down.

I wobble down the back steps, in no hurry. I hear something in the basement, a rat maybe, won't be the first time, whatever I might have told that girl. But it's the boys, Simon and Wesley. I smile and wave, do my best to put them at ease. They're good boys. I feel them watching me as I unlock the storeroom.

"Just temporary," I say. I pull out my wallet, give them each a buck. "Our secret." But they're already off and squeaking up the steps.

If I lie down, I may never get up. It's as simple as that. I hold onto the shelves for balance, rattling the empty bottles I've stashed, but still drop to the mattress with a thud. I lay my head on the pillow, close my eyes, picture Shelley, and wonder if she would have me if she knew.

There's a tap at the open door and when I look up I see the Turk and his wife. I thought they were gone for good, but there they are towering over me in my storeroom. She's sniffling and he's rubbing her shoulders like she's a prize-fighter between rounds. Now he's got his pen out and he's writing in the air as if he's practicing his signature. And right behind them is Shelley, her cheery, ignorant smile shining blissfully down.

"We want the place," Kemal told Artoyen. The old guy went pale.

And when Bettina nodded and put her arm through Kemal's, she thought Sam was going to have a stroke.

Never accept as true that which may be a profitable lie.

"Look," I tell them as Kemal helps me stand, "I might have been wrong about the schools."

"I tried to call," Shelley says. She's not looking at me, though. Her eyes are on the mattress and the suitcase.

"It's not what you think," I say to Shelley, looking past the young couple.

"What I hear is that they used to be pretty good," I say to the girl, "but these days they're lousy with gangs, even drugs."

"You don't look well, Sammy," says Shelley. "Is something wrong?"

"There's a good explanation, Shell," I say, and even while my mind is spinning the story I'll tell her, the elaborate lie that will hide my flaws for one more day, I know the simple truth is what she needs.

"Did you hear us?" Kemal asks. "We're ready to sign."

I put my arm around Kemal's shoulders, and move him, a step at a time, to the stairs. I'm practically whispering, the most sincere voice I've got. "You don't want your kid in a school like that, do you?" A dose of truth for the Turk, too. "The contractors cut a few too many corners. The place is a money pit. And the artists! Don't get me started about the artists."

My heart is running like a mad dog and I know it's going to explode. I can't believe I just let these kids walk out the door, when that sale was going to save my ass. When there's no way Shelley will have me, now that she knows about the closet. I ought to call little Sammy, make things right. Maybe ask Connie if we can't work something out financially. Beg Shelley to forgive me, tell her everything.

But it's all so complicated, how my world works, how it gets twisted around. If it were simple, if life weren't full of cracks and holes, huge gaps that need to be filled, I wouldn't have to invent. And as I feel my knees slip out from under me, the floor rushing up, I wonder where the truth lies.

THE REPLACEMENT WIFE

Women her age aren't supposed to need hysterectomies. That's for older women, her mother, her aunt. In her family of hardy Chinese immigrants, it's almost a rite of passage. But not yet. Not for her. It's too soon.

When Jessica's doctor had told her the procedure was recommended for women with endometriosis, even with her relatively mild symptoms—painful cramps, an ache in her lower back that some days felt like a hot stove—she dismissed the idea as absurd. She hadn't yet reached thirty, she intended to marry and have children, at least two. A hysterectomy was out of the question. And yet here was this doctor, a perfectly credible OB/GYN, with multiple diplomas and certificates on the wall of her office and a calm, confident demeanor, telling her that none of that was going to happen, that it was best to deal with the problem sooner rather than later, before it developed into something surgery might not be able to resolve.

Jessica wishes she had someone to talk to, but there's no one. No big sister to lean on, no cousins she's in touch with. She has friends, of course. The girls from the bookstore where she works would listen politely for a while, but they're even younger than she is, more aware of their tattoos and piercings than their reproductive organs. They wouldn't understand. There's Lorraine, her college roommate, but she's in Cleveland, and calling her is a gamble. The last time they'd spoken, Lorraine was in one of her depressed funks, barely coherent. That's not what Jessica needs.

She obviously can't tell Feng-qi, although they've reached the stage in their relationship where they're discussing intimate matters, self-doubts, even preferred sexual positions. She'd been relieved after their first time in bed together, when they talked about what had happened. Not in any bizarre ego-boosting way aimed at him, but about practical things: pace and angles, the finish, the cleanup. Although she'd expected him to be something of a prude—he'd grown up in China, after all, not in sex-crazed America—he'd shown no hesitancy to discuss these things and make adjustments. No other man she'd slept with had been so forthright and responsive. Was that something his late wife Maddie had taught him? The prep-school girl and Berkeley grad, rebellious daughter of privilege, auto-accident fatality? Jessica guessed it was. He would have gotten that openness from her.

But this is different. This is about Jessica's wholeness, about her ability to bear Feng-qi's children, assuming that's what he wants, assuming they will indeed marry, assuming so many goddamn things that she can't keep track of all the variables. This is about her whole life. And who can understand that?

She wishes she could speak to her mother. But she's never been able to talk of such things with her mother, dating from girlhood days when she was simply expected to know what was happening to her body, and questions she summoned the courage to raise were dismissed without answers. Tampons had suddenly appeared in her room one day, a pamphlet in black and white explaining what they were for, along with an illustrated guide to resisting boys' advances.

Jessica had resolved then to do a better job of helping her own daughter, when the time came, through menstruation and sex and birth control and all of the other mysteries of young womanhood about which she'd been left to puzzle on her own. But now, apparently, that isn't going to happen.

Jessica picks up Feng-qi's younger son, Wesley, from preschool and listens to him talk about his day, although, in her distracted muddle, little registers. They arrive at Feng-qi's apartment at the edge of D.C.'s Chinatown to wait for Simon to get home from first grade. Feng-qi's father is puttering in the kitchen when they enter.

"Are you well, Lao Zhang?" she asks him in her limited Chinese, freeing Wesley to run to his room. *Lao* is a term of respect, she understands, although she's uncomfortable calling anyone old. He has been ill for weeks, which is why she's been pressed into childcare duty.

"*Heng hao*," he answers. Very well. But then he coughs and bends to spit in the sink.

Simon buzzes into the apartment and dumps his book satchel on the living room floor; Wesley races back downstairs to greet him. Both boys climb onto stools at the kitchen counter for a snack.

"Can we have cookies?" Simon asks.

"Yeah, cookies," Wesley says.

When she first started spending time with the family—visiting for the occasional meal, tagging along on outings—the boys mostly ignored her. Even if she tried to engage them by asking a question about school or some cartoon she was sure they watched, they would feign deafness, or babble nonsense to each other, or direct their responses not to her but to their father. She'd understood their resentment. They'd lost their mother, and she was an interloper. It had stung, but she understood. Now they seem to accept her, or tolerate her, which amounts to the same thing for boys their ages. They let her read to them. They let her wipe their noses when necessary. They let her prepare snacks. They draw the line at snuggling, a pleasure she's not sure she's prepared for anyway, but perhaps that, too, would come in time.

The boys finish their cookies and milk and run off to their rooms while she boils water for Lao Zhang's tea.

Lao Zhang is even tougher to get through to than the boys. Since his arrival from Shanghai, she's seen him struggle. He can only communicate easily with Feng-qi, although he's picked up a fair amount of basic English from the boys. Jessica's Chinese has improved, too, something she never thought would happen. Growing up in Los Angeles it was the last thing she wanted to learn, and she'd only acquired those words that her parents, immigrants from Taiwan doing their best to assimilate, incorporated into their own brand of pidgin.

Maddie's mother, the boys' maternal grandmother, is a frequent visitor to the Zhang home, and Jessica briefly considers talking to her about the surgery, but discussing anything with Mrs. Martin is awkward. Something this personal would be out of the question. Although the boys had never met their grandmother until after their mother's accident, they love it when she comes down from Connecticut. She's their link to Maddie, even though she's retained some of her initial stiffness toward them and their father. She's at least learned to bring presents for the boys and to eat with chopsticks and to drink green, instead of black, tea. She's more comfortable with the whole family now. Except for her late daughter's husband's girlfriend.

But Jessica can't keep quiet about her problem for long. She knows that Feng-qi is going to propose marriage soon. That's where their relationship has been headed from the beginning, and she's done nothing to stop it. She knows what Feng-qi is thinking and she knows the complications. She is to be the replacement wife. She wants to be married, and

Feng-qi is a good man, but the death of the beloved Maddie will hang over them for years, maybe forever. Feng-qi has told Jessica that he feels sometimes Maddie is present, that she watches over the boys, that she hovers nearby. Can Jessica tell him how that frightens her? To know that everything she does, everything she says, is being watched? To sleep in Feng-qi's bed with Maddie in the room? Even if she doesn't believe—but how could she not, with several millennia of Chinese superstitions telling her otherwise—it's enough that Feng-qi believes.

And, ghost or not, the household is imprinted with Maddie. "Mommy doesn't read it that way," Simon has said more than once, when Jessica fails to provide characters in his books with distinct, funny voices. "That's not how Mommy makes the bed." Wesley is too little to know, but he's begun to say the same things. "This oatmeal doesn't taste like Mommy's."

On top of all that, both boys have made it clear to Jessica that their mother is coming back. They have learned about resurrection in Sunday school, although of course they don't know the word for it, and they're convinced it could happen. Sometimes when Simon comes home from school he wanders around the apartment, looking into rooms and closets as though he expects to find her. Before bed, Wesley occasionally asks if Mommy will be home for breakfast. And so, if Jessica is there, if Jessica lives in the same room with their father, sleeping in the same bed, won't it be harder for their mother to come back? Won't she be angry that there's no place for her?

Jessica understands all this. It makes her want to run as far away as she can, but she understands.

Lao Zhang, on the other hand, doesn't bear the same resentment. He had not known Maddie and is only living in the U.S. with Feng-qi and the boys because she's gone. In a way, Jessica and the old man are two feet filling the same shoe, and she's grown fond of him. He reminds her of her own father, with his stray chin hairs and yellow teeth, the way his nose whistles when he sleeps. But Lao Zhang is failing. She sees this in his drooping, sallow skin, his hoarse speech, his unsteady hands. He sits in his room and sips the tea she brings to him, or ignores it, while he gazes out the window at the dusty alley, or at something beyond.

When Feng-qi comes home from work, he and Jessica cook together what she has begun to assemble for the family dinner. She waits with the boys while Feng-qi carries a tray to his father, and then they eat—part, not even all, of a makeshift family. They are a puzzle, and the pieces don't fit. She doesn't belong, and yet Feng-qi will propose. It will be soon, she knows. Before Lao Zhang . . . before long, Feng-qi will want to settle the matter. Make the arrangements. And she will have to decide.

The operation is scheduled. She still hasn't told Feng-qi, although he certainly could have noticed the symptoms. The bleeding has become heavier lately, as she was told it would, the cramps debilitating. Some days the pain is unbearable, a torment of fire, and she can only expect more of the same. But will the cure be worse?

Feng-qi suggests dinner out, just the two of them. Lao Zhang will watch the boys, and Claudia, their haughty but dependable neighbor, will stop by to check on things. It's obvious what's coming. Jessica knows there will be a ring, a question she should be prepared to answer. She knows she should tell him that Maddie's presence makes her uncomfortable. She knows she should tell him about the surgery. Even with all this knowledge, she has no idea what to do.

The restaurant he's chosen is Mario's, the site of their first real date. They're Chinese, he lives in Chinatown, they cook Chinese at home, but they both like Italian food when they eat out and this—so he declared, although Jessica doesn't remember being consulted—is their restaurant. All signs say this is the night.

She decides to forestall him. She will eat, she will talk about the boys and Lao Zhang and poor Claudia, their neighbor who lost her job, and the baby Susanna down the hall is expecting—or no, maybe not the baby, she doesn't want to talk about babies—and she will be thoroughly pleasant and charming. But, if he reaches into his pocket, if it looks like he's about to launch into a serious topic, if he mentions the future, she will stop him. She will say, "Feng," because she sometimes calls him Feng, the wind, "there's something you should know." And she'll tell him about the endometriosis and the hysterectomy and what it means for them, and she will give him a chance to leave the ring in the box, safely tucked away in his pocket. She'll save him the embarrassment of having to rescind his proposal when he learns the truth. She's doing them both a big favor. And if he doesn't reach into his pocket, if the conversation stays light and superficial, she'll phone him one day next week to tell him she's in the hospital, nothing to worry about. She won't even tell him which hospital, because the last thing she's going to want is the Zhang family arriving with flowers and balloons when she's just had her insides scraped out. When she leaves the hospital she'll go home, or she'll visit her parents, or she'll get away somewhere. She'll gradually disappear from the lives of Feng-qi and his sons and Lao Zhang, because that's what's best for them all.

The salads come and go, the pasta, the dessert. Feng-qi pays the check and they're strolling down Seventh Street. The night ends.

She postpones the surgery.

Lao Zhang is weaker. Feng-qi takes him to doctors, including a clinic in Chinatown where one of the nurses speaks

Shanghainese, but it isn't clear what's wrong. One doctor suggests that the old man misses China, that a trip back home might be good for him. Another says it's city life that's the problem, that he needs to visit the countryside. It becomes increasingly difficult to leave the boys alone with him, which brings back the whole issue of childcare that caused Feng-qi to go to Shanghai to bring his father to America in the first place. Maddie's mother agrees to extend her visits, and that helps some. Claudia, jobless and depending on the vagaries of freelance work to support herself, seems to appreciate the extra dollars that paid childcare brings her, and that fills the gaps. But Jessica suspects that everyone—Simon and Wesley, Lao Zhang, Mrs. Martin, Claudia, Feng-qi, probably even Maddie, wherever she might be—is looking at her, the replacement wife, as the long-term solution to the problem.

Jessica and Feng-qi go out to eat again, this time to a *tapas* bar on Seventh. It's loud, a fun spot, not romantic, no danger of a proposal here. None of the worry has disappeared, but for one night it can recede.

"Lao Zhang is doing better, I think," says Jessica while they're waiting for their meal to arrive. He isn't, but she thinks Feng-qi needs to hear it anyway.

"Yes. I think so, too."

"The music here is good," she says, because no other topic seems safe. "I love the Gypsy Kings."

"Yes," he says.

Between dinner and dessert, Jessica visits the ladies' room. She makes her way back through a bustle of waiters and patrons, and, when she gets to the table and is about to sit, she sees a small black box next to a steaming cup of espresso. With her hands gripping the back of the chair, the noise of the place suddenly louder, the music and the voices, she looks at the box. A painful lump forms in her throat. Her scheme to evade the question has been thwarted. She can't look at Feng-qi, but out of the corner of her eye she sees his hand reach toward her. She pulls her hand away, turns and runs, bangs into a waiter and ricochets into a busboy, toppling his stacked tray of plates and glasses. The crash of dishes and cutlery, the shrieks of startled diners, the complaint of the busboy and waiter—all echo together as she pushes out of the restaurant. She doesn't stop to see if Feng-qi follows. She thinks she hears him call her name but doesn't turn around. She runs toward Pennsylvania Avenue, away from Feng-qi, away from Nanking Mansion.

She calls the next day and asks him to meet her in a coffee shop. It's familiar to them both and feels neutral, comfortable. When she enters, Feng-qi is waiting.

"About last night," she begins, "I'm sorry." She wants him to stop her, to say that no explanation is necessary, but he *doesn't* stop her and clearly an explanation *is* necessary. "I kind of freaked."

"Yes," he says.

Over the years he's been in America, he has nearly perfected his English, but he still doesn't always say the right thing. Now, he doesn't joke about her apology although she wishes he would. He doesn't laugh, or say, "you sure did," or "you got that right." Nor does he soften his acknowledgement of her admission with "I wouldn't say that," or "I understand." Instead, he's honest and blunt: "Yes."

"I wanted to explain."

"We talked about this," Feng-qi says. "I thought it was what you wanted."

"It was. It is."

The problem is the surgery. She's been up all night thinking about it, and that's the conclusion she's come to. Of course she wants to marry him. He's a wonderful man. Distinguished. Smart. Great with his kids. *His* kids, although in time . . . She's seen how loving he is with his father and respectful with

Mrs. Martin. He works hard. He's even Chinese, which her mother had long ago given up hoping for.

So it had to be the surgery that was bothering her, and it wasn't fair to him not to explain.

"The thing is," she says, "I have to tell you something." Oh, God, it sounds so melodramatic, like she might be about to admit she's an escaped convict, a serial killer, or worse. "And when I do, I'll completely understand if you don't want to marry me."

Feng-qi's face grows a worried expression, the eyes turned down, narrow and serious. He reaches for her trembling hand, which this time she lets him take. She tells him about the endometriosis, the pain, the bleeding that's been getting worse, and the recommended treatment. He doesn't know the word in English. She has to explain the excruciating details of what will be done to her body, what's going to be removed. What it means for the future.

When she finishes and settles into a damp-eyed silence, looking not at him but at her own hand in his, he pulls the little box from his pocket and places it in front of her. This time she opens it.

She's in George Washington University Hospital for four days. Feng-qi brings her home, his home, her future home, and sets her up in his room, while he moves to the living room couch. She protests that one invalid in the house is enough—Lao Zhang now rarely leaves his bed—but in truth, she's grateful. She has nowhere else to go, no one else to help her recover. She still doesn't want to talk about the implications of what has been done to her, but she doesn't want to be alone either.

Feng-qi hires Claudia, who arrives early to make breakfast for the whole family, gets the boys ready for school, and looks after both Jessica and Lao Zhang until Feng-qi comes home in the evening. The boys, having been warned to be quiet so both patients can rest, take their responsibility seriously, and Jessica barely hears them.

At the start of her second week of convalescence, she wakes to see Simon and Wesley standing at the door of her room—Feng-qi's room.

"Your eyes are open," Simon says.

"Are they?" she asks, and both boys nod.

"Ye-Ye likes us to read to him when he's sick," Simon says, holding up his book to show her. Ye-Ye is what they call Lao Zhang.

Jessica pats the bed, and the boys, thus freed from their vows of silence, noisily race to hop up. Simon lands with a whoop between her and Wesley.

"Once upon a time," Simon begins, even before he opens the book.

In time, she recovers. Although Claudia still visits each day, Jessica feels useless and takes over some of the lighter household duties. She makes breakfast. She dusts. She wonders what she is supposed to do. Should she go?

One evening after Feng-qi gets home, while the boys are in their room and Lao Zhang is in his, she perches on a stool in the kitchen while he prepares dinner.

"I'm feeling better," she says.

He looks at her over the measuring cup filled with rice. "Good."

"So I suppose I should leave."

He adds the rice to a pot of water, checks the gas flame on the burner, and moves to the cutting board where he picks up the cleaver and, in one swift move, splits a green pepper. "There's no hurry," he says, dicing the halves. Then he turns to her. "Is there?"

He hasn't pressed her to go, or to set a date for the wedding, or to do anything. They haven't even told the boys that they're engaged. She waits for it now, the question of when, has she given thought to this, made arrangements for that, but he's chopping and stirring and asks nothing.

Each day she's a little stronger. She's ambulatory now, but hasn't yet gone back to work. The manager of the bookstore has been generous beyond expectation. She's welcome back whenever she's ready, and she thinks the time has nearly come. Lao Zhang needs little attention, sleeping as he does most of each day. She reads, and she finds that she is drawn to Maddie's dog-eared favorites: Austen, Eliot, the Brontës. She studies Chinese halfheartedly, practicing the strokes for each character over and over again until her mind has drifted and she no longer has any idea what the pictograph means. She leaves the apartment to walk up and down the hallway Gallery, and tries to make sense of the paintings that hang there. These excursions wear her out, at first, but then it isn't long before she strolls the block in front of Nanking Mansion, watching the leaves on the maples turn, watching one house decay, another, swarmed by workmen inside and out, revive. She tries a loop, turning the corner and passing through the alley, until one day she is confronted by two neighborhood toughs. After that, she confines her exercise to M Street, down to the corner and back.

Returning from one such stroll, she notices that the door to the building's front unit is open. The girl who works at the coffee shop, Susanna, has recently had her baby and moved from that unit into the back apartment with Aloysius. Jessica has spoken to neither, but in these weeks of lying alone in Feng-qi's bed she has heard the baby's cries, has tried to tune them out, has failed to erase the baby from her thoughts.

Cautiously, because she's curious about the owner of the apartment, a famous writer who has not long ago returned from France, she approaches his door and peeks inside. The man is sitting at his kitchen table.

He looks up just as she steps into view. "Mei-ling!"

She lurches back, looking for someplace to hide, but there is no escape. "I'm so sorry," she says. "I'm Jessica Lee. I live,"—she points vaguely down the hallway—"that is, I'm visiting the Zhangs."

"Of course. The boys. Sad."

"Yes."

The man is not as old as she'd thought. His eyes are sharp and dark, his hair, slate and ash, is swept back. He invites her in and they drink tea. She admits that she's not read his books, although, having worked in a bookstore, she's read widely. She tells him about her current obsession with the Nineteenth Century writers, but she also loves Kingsolver, Atwood, Tan. Novels by men intimidate her, she says, although as soon as the words leave her mouth she wonders if that's true.

"I think," she says, trying to explain, "that I don't understand men."

He nods as if she's uttered something profound. He rises, retrieves one of his own novels. On the cover is a photograph of a boat. The photograph on the back is of a younger version of the writer: thicker hair, slimmer waist.

"It's a love story," he says. "In the end, they're all just love stories."

She reads the book, keeping it hidden from Feng-qi, although she can't say why. It's about an all-consuming love of a man for a woman, one that shreds the man's soul when his wife dies. Does passion like that exist in real life? Feng-qi is a good man, but she doesn't feel that way about him, and she knows he doesn't feel it for her. But is that what he had with Maddie? Is the hurt he experienced when she died so deep that he'll never recover? Or will there come a time when the two of them grow into such a connection? Isn't that what every woman wants? She is weeping when she reads the final words of the book, and she begins again.

A few days later, she knocks on the writer's door to return the book, and again he invites her in for tea.

"I couldn't put it down," she says. He hasn't asked for a reaction, but Jessica is still amazed that the book's protagonist could feel so much. "When he set fire to the boat, I cried."

"That's the difference between men and women. Men become angry that he is in such pain over a woman. They think he should get in the boat and sail away. But that's not a real ending. That's a recipe for heartache."

"This way he deals with it, doesn't he?" she says. "He doesn't mope around forever trying to recover what he's lost. It's cathartic."

"Exactly," he says.

She visits every afternoon, before the boys come home. She showers, puts on make-up, a drop of perfume. Dressing is difficult because she hasn't brought much from her own apartment, but she tries to wear something different each time, or a different combination: jeans and her white blouse with a sweater one day, a shawl the next. She checks on Lao Zhang before she leaves and slips through the Gallery to the writer's apartment.

As the days pass she grows stronger, the pain less demanding of her attention. She can't justify her continued presence at Nanking Mansion, but she makes no preparations to return home.

One evening at dinner, while the boys are telling their father about school, about a playground incident or something else that barely registers on Jessica's consciousness, she is thinking of Nathan, the writer. On her visit that afternoon he told her she was beautiful, that she looked regal.

"Are you feeling all right?" Feng-qi asks.

She realizes that he and the boys are staring at her. Her untouched rice and stir-fried vegetables have grown cold on her plate, but she feels heat rise in her face as if she has been caught in a lie.

"Yes. I mean, no, not really. I think I'll lie down." And she knows they are watching her as she climbs the stairs to the bedroom.

Nathan asks if she would read pages from his new book. He's especially interested in her perspective as a Chinese woman. His second wife was also Chinese, he explains, and then fills her in on his less-than-admirable marital record. The next morning, after Feng-qi has left for work, she reads the account of a family destroyed by the Nanjing Massacre, of slaughtered infants and women, of the thousands of lost souls that now wander in search of their families. That afternoon, she returns the pages and he tells her more about his novel tracing the history of atrocity.

"It's about silence," he says. "It's about the obligation to speak."

She tells him what she knows of the massacre, although her parents have not talked to her about it, and as far as she knows her family was not affected. They fled to Taiwan in '49 from their native Sichuan Province to escape a different set of horrors. He makes notes as they talk and the next day he shows her revised pages.

While she reads, silently turning the manuscript pages on the table, he takes her hand.

"No," she says, tugging free.

"I'm sorry," he says. "It's just that you remind me . . ."

When she leaves, she lingers by the door. He comes to her, lifts her hand to his lips, kisses it. And then he kisses her mouth. She's told him she is engaged to Feng-qi, that she will soon become his wife and stepmother to the Zhang boys, but still he kisses her. She lets him kiss her.

As a little girl in L.A., along with all of her little-girl friends, Jessica dreamed of a big wedding, in a church filled with flowers, followed by a lavish reception attended by movie stars. Never realistic, given her parents' modest means, that dream has long since faded. Now, as the preparations for her real wedding proceed, she thinks small, mixing Chinese and Western traditions. It will be more party than religious rite, more passage than destination.

Feng-qi has left all the arrangements to her. She secures a hall at the Chinatown community center. She has invitations printed, hires a caterer who claims he can do both dim sum and hors d'oeuvres.

Every day she meets with Nathan and they work on his book. He asks more about her heritage, of which she knows too little, and teaches her not only about the Japanese atrocities in China, but also about Mao's disastrous policies, about famine and genocide, about the Cultural Revolution. Each day as she leaves in time to greet the boys after school, she lets him kiss her.

"Feng," she says, almost whispering his name. They are in the living room, each reading in the glow of a table lamp. He looks up, marking his place with a finger. "Would it be okay if we postpone?" She's talking about the wedding, of course, but she can't bring herself to say the word. She waits for a reaction, but the blankness of his expression, like a cloudless sky, says everything.

"It's just that maybe I'm not totally recovered. From the surgery." A thud, followed by laughter, reverberates from the boys' room. A fly bounces noisily inside the lampshade. "Another month or two should do it."

"If you think that's best," he says, and returns to his book.

It isn't that she wants him to argue with her, to somehow prove that he really does want to marry her. He's a patient man, and that's as much a part of love as passion is. But she needs to be blamed. She needs to be accused so that she can defend herself and argue with him, so that she can purge the guilt that has filled the empty place inside.

Outside, the air has turned cold when, months after her visits with Nathan began, she lets him take her to bed. Mentally, she longs for him. Physically, though, since the operation, she feels no desire, feels more like a mannequin than a woman, a stand-in for the real thing. But Nathan has been so kind and gentle, urgent in his kisses yet respectful of her reluctance, and she wants to please him. She is ready now when he undresses her. She lets him explore her with his hands, tries not to flinch when he enters her first with his fingers, tries not to cry out in pain. She moves him away, onto his back, and then straddles him, eases herself onto him, pushing up when the pain comes, slipping down, then up again, until her body grows accustomed to the new sensation and she can make a gentle rhythm for them both.

Every afternoon it is the same, and soon the pain subsides. She knows what she can tolerate and what she cannot. A kind of pleasure returns.

One afternoon after being with Nathan, Jessica returns to the Zhang apartment to find that the boys are already home from school. Lao Zhang sits on the couch in his pajamas and slippers. His face is drained and his hands shake.

"You go out?" he asks.

"Yes," she says. "To visit a friend."

"Boys come home."

"I'm sorry."

Lao Zhang says no more, and she helps him back to bed. When Feng-qi gets home after work, she wonders what the old man will tell him. As they make dinner, peeling and chopping and frying, she feels the engagement ring on her hand and wants to tell him about Nathan. Or, rather, she wants *not* to tell him about Nathan, but that she can't go through with the wedding.

When she opens her mouth to speak, watching steam rise from the boiling rice, the scent of the onions hits her, and tears form in her eyes. Her body aches. She can't say the words.

That night, instead of sleeping on the couch, as he as been doing since he brought her to the apartment after her surgery, Feng-qi comes into her room, his room, and slips into bed next to her.

At dinner the next night, Feng-qi looks at Jessica and clears his throat. "Boys," he says, although his eyes are still on her, "we have something to tell you."

Jessica looks down at her plate, on the mound of rice that isn't like Maddie used to make, and the snow peas that aren't like Maddie used to make, and the soy sauce and oil that congeal between them like blood.

"I know you boys still miss your mother very much. So do I. But Jessica and I are going to get married. And she's going to live here with us."

Jessica expects the boys to protest, to scream or run to their room and slam doors, to insist that their mother will come back. But instead they stare at their father, a reflection of his own blank expression.

After dinner, as Jessica and Feng-qi do the dishes, he asks, "Have you picked a date?"

"Yes," she says, without hesitation, and she names a date.

"Good," he says.

This time there is no rented room, no invitations. Partly because Lao Zhang is so ill and partly because Jessica cannot bear to make her deception so public—she has continued to see Nathan each afternoon while Feng-qi is at work—they are married at City Hall. After the event, they host a reception in the apartment that spills out into the Gallery.

Susanna and Aloysius are there, one or the other of them checking frequently on the baby. Claudia is there, but she spends most of her time looking after Simon and Wesley. The sculptor is there, and the painter. Also the school teacher and the decorator. Everyone in the building comes. When Nathan appears, Jessica avoids him. She knows she should say something to him, neighborly pleasantries, anything, but she can't. Instead, she takes Feng-qi's arm, feeds him a bite of wedding cake, turns her back to the guests.

She returns to work. The surgery now feels like a bad dream, one that haunts her when she remembers what has been taken from her, that she is less than a woman now. But mostly it is repressed, and she is too busy to let it surface. Feng-qi has invited her to add her own touches to the apartment, to pick out new furniture or move things from her old apartment, to repaint. They can all do it together, he offers, to put their mark on the place as a family, but she'll be in charge of the project. She picks up catalogs from Crate & Barrel, from Pottery Barn and Restoration Hardware, and they all page through them. Lao Zhang selects a low cherry cabinet to replace the altar table he's made in the living room. The boys at first choose beds that look like race cars, but Jessica is able to convince them that a double desk with shelving for books and games will be more practical. Feng-qi says he wants nothing, but she notices that he lingers over a particular arm-chair covered in a plush red fabric. She also studies the catalogs, but nothing grabs her interest. All of the catalogs migrate to a drawer in an end table. She places no orders.

On a cold, dark day, after Feng-qi has gone into the office and the boys have gone off to school, and Lao Zhang is settled on the sofa in the living room with his tea and comforter, she sets off for work. The trees are bare and the wind whistles through the swaying branches. She turns the corner onto

Seventh Street and is startled by the flashing red lights of three police cars and a fire truck. Two vehicles, one a black Mercedes and one so rumpled that she can't identify it, sit in the center of the road as if locked in an embrace. The windshield of the Mercedes is marred by a gaping round moon surrounded by waves of shattered glass, like ripples in a pond. Spectators have gathered to watch the extraction of the victims. They point and whisper. Jessica turns away and stumbles to the curb, where she sinks.

The sound of breaking glass reaches her, the cry of metal stretched, shouted instructions, horrified gasps. She thinks of Maddie and her accident, the gaping hole in the Zhang family that Jessica is meant to fill. Her stomach convulses and she vomits in the street.

She stands, unsteadily, and totters back to Nanking Mansion. She will call the store, tell them she's had a relapse. Already embarrassed by what she's told them about her surgery, they won't ask questions now. She'll call again tomorrow and the next day and eventually she'll tell them she isn't going back.

She climbs the steps into the building and stops in the Gallery. At the end of the hall is her home, where she lives with her new family, her husband and sons. In the center are the abstract paintings, like windows to the unknown. And at the front of the building, in the apartment with a view of the gray, cold street, is Nathan. Behind the door he works on his book, or reads, or sleeps. It doesn't matter what he does so much as what he could do, what he understands about her, about the world. She listens to the wind howl outside. And then she takes a step, and knocks on Nathan's door.

THE SHRINE TO HIS ANCESTORS

Zhang Feng-qi kneels before the low table in the corner. Left of center, he assembles a pyramid of oranges: a triangle of three and one nesting on top. He lifts and dusts with his sleeve a photograph of Maddie, his late wife and the mother of his two sons. In the picture, one he'd taken on their honeymoon trip to Chicago, her blond hair swirls around her face and she is hugging her jacket to keep it tight against the wind. Her smile is wide. He remembers the moment. They were happy, he deliriously so. Before the wedding, her mother had been angry that she was marrying Feng-qi (not, he later realized, because he was Chinese, but because he was other—any other). And his parents were thousands of miles away in Shanghai, equally disappointed in his choice. But at that moment, clowning in front of the larger-than-life lions of the Art Institute, they didn't care what anyone else thought.

He replaces that picture on the table and picks up another. This one is of his mother, who died years ago. He believes the photograph was taken by his father on the Bund in Shanghai, but the blurry crowd in the background could have arisen anywhere in that dense city. She is stiffly posed, aware of the camera and forcing a smile; her gray-streaked hair is pulled back. A dull blue jacket in the old Party style makes her shoulders look wide and strong, which Feng-qi knows they were not. There's also an older sepia print of his father and mother together in what might be their wedding finery. The last photograph, of his father, is more recent, taken after he'd moved here to D.C. from China just last year. Feng-qi wishes he had chosen a different picture, because here his father looks nervous and uncomfortable, as if thinking he should have remained in Shanghai to finish his days among the bones of his forebears, but in all the other snapshots he appears drawn and sick, with the inevitable too clearly published on his tired face.

Feng-qi lights the stick of incense, watches the drifting string of smoke rise, and inhales the scent of sandalwood that he will forever associate with his father. The shrine had been the old man's creation, his link to the ancient ways. Feng-qi doesn't believe in such things. And yet, the memories abide here and they comfort him. He bows to the pictures, and rises.

From next door comes a steady hammering noise: the long-delayed renovation project in his neighbor's apartment. A gaping hole in the brick wall facing the alley, the origin of which Feng-qi no longer remembers, is to be repaired and a balcony installed. The balcony seems unsafe for Susanna's baby, who will soon begin to crawl, but Feng-qi understands (because six-year-old Simon has told him this) that Aloysius plans to sell the apartment and move, with Susanna and little Loyal, to a quieter, safer community. Which, Feng-qi supposes, would be anywhere that Thomas—the father of the baby and the man with whom Susanna used to live, and who even now often sits in his parked car on M Street watching the building—is less likely to follow. And if he does follow, like the hungry ghost of Chinese legends, what then?

Claudia, their neighbor and, lately, the boys' sitter, enters with Simon and Wesley, who both run to Feng-qi to show him what they have found on their walk. Simon presents him with a handful of leaves, ordinary maple and oak leaves that show signs of the changing season, still green but gold and red at the edges. Wesley clutches a dandelion that he holds under his chin, as Claudia has apparently instructed him.

"Yellow," says Wesley.

"It certainly is," says Feng-qi.

"They both wanted to bring you presents," Claudia says.

Feng-qi would be lost without Claudia, a former marketing consultant who has taken readily to childcare and now seems content only when she's around the boys. These past months, as his father sank out of reach, Feng-qi had struggled to care for Simon and Wesley, just as he had after Maddie's car accident. When he'd married Jessica, second-generation Chinese-American with her own family ties to the old country, he thought she'd be able to help more, that they would face his father's death together and carry the boys through yet another loss. That wasn't why he married her; he just thought it would be so. But she's been distracted, busy with her work, and more uncomfortable with the boys, and they with her, than he'd hoped. He believes harmony will come in time, because that's what his father had taught him. He just doesn't know when.

Now there is high-pitched barking in the hallway and they all—Feng-qi, Claudia, and the boys—go to investigate the commotion. Charles and Craig, from Number 1, reunited after a brief separation, are assembled there with their pug Sascha and a new dog they have named Mole, pronounced, Claudia has explained because it is a Spanish word Feng-qi doesn't understand, "molay." The new dog is meant to keep Sascha company and to replace—if replacement is the right notion, which Feng-qi knows it is not—their first pug who, Charles and Craig maintain, was dog-napped.

Shelley, Mr. Artoyen's buxom new wife, comes out of their apartment, shushing as she eases the door shut, because Sam, as he insists everyone call him now that he is just one of the residents instead of being the building's developer, is recovering from the heart attack he suffered while they were moving in. The painter, the wiry little man with the gray eyes, peeks out of his unit, releasing a wave of paint fumes that bites at Feng-qi's nose. The man emerges, carrying a painting—awkwardly balanced on his hip, arms stretched to their limits because it is a long, wide canvas—that he lifts onto oversized hooks that have been empty for months. Aiding in this effort—mostly by judging from afar whether the canvas hangs level—is the tall sculptor from Number 3 whose ubiquitous cigarette dangles, unlit, from his mouth. The work looks familiar to Feng-qi, as if the painter has recreated the piece that once hung in that spot, an indecipherable abstract roofline under an impossibly blue sky.

The chaos in the hallway Gallery reminds Feng-qi of the day his mother-in-law—Maddie's mother—had arrived unannounced, the day of his first date with Jessica, the day his father remembered was the anniversary of the Nanjing Massacre. The day Feng-qi realized that, no matter how much he planned, no matter how settled he thought he was, his life was an ocean of change over which he had no control.

And just as this thought occurs to him, he sees through the Gallery's glass doors a yellow cab pull up and Mrs. Martin emerge, as if his memory has conjured her appearance. He has forgotten that she was due, but regular visits are now her custom. Despite his marriage to Jessica, she has been coming each month since his father's funeral, whether because his death foretells her own and she wishes to make the most of the time remaining to her, or because she genuinely wants to help, he can't be sure. It hardly matters. The boys see her now, pull the door open and welcome her with noisy hugs and kisses, which she tolerates with grace that a year ago was unthinkable. She greets Feng-qi by patting his forearm with a gloved hand.

The door to the building's front apartment opens and now, he thinks, the tableau will be complete, exactly as it was that day. But of course the young couple who once lived there is a couple no more and have left that apartment. It is the famous novelist who lives there now, the writer who, Jessica has told him, has a great book that is about to be published. At this time last year the man was in Paris, but his return to Nanking Mansion has sown more change, more chaos. However, instead of the novelist emerging from the apartment, as Feng-qi expects, it is Jessica who closes the door behind her.

Jessica and Mrs. Martin stand face to face. The two women are roughly the same height, but the similarity ends there. Jessica's black hair hangs straight to her shoulders and her dark complexion is, or to Feng-qi's eye appears to be, without makeup. Mrs. Martin's hair is gray, rigidly swirled above her head like a crown, and her powdered face is pale. Jessica wears jeans and a t-shirt. Mrs. Martin is in a black suit. If there is resentment between them, neither has said so to Feng-qi. And yet they do not speak. They simply nod.

And then the commotion in the Gallery dissipates. Charles and Craig and the dogs depart for their afternoon walk; the painter, his new work now hanging, returns to his studio, as does the sculptor. The hammering from the back of the building has ceased, along with the crying. And Claudia and Mrs. Martin herd Simon and Wesley into the Zhangs' apartment for a promised snack and a glimpse at the presents their grandmother has brought. Only Feng-qi and Jessica remain.

"You were in the writer's apartment," Feng-qi says. He has learned in his few months of marriage to Jessica that questions are often misinterpreted, and so he usually speaks to her in statements. He doesn't mean to accuse her. He only seeks confirmation of a fact.

"You saw me come out," Jessica says.

"He was there." Although in intonation this is also a statement, in his mind he is asking a question. He didn't see the writer. He doesn't know whether it is true.

"We were going over his manuscript one last time."

Jessica has told him that the book is done. When she quit her job at the bookstore—she said after her hysterectomy that she couldn't stand the way people looked at her there, a young woman who was no longer a woman—she began working with the writer to help him finish his book about atrocities. She has told Feng-qi that part of the book involves China, especially the Japanese massacre of Chinese civilians at Nanjing in 1937. Feng-qi knows about this incident, of course. His father survived it although he never talked about it. The massacre is part of his own family history and he doesn't understand why it should be put in a book of fiction.

"The book is finished." A question and a statement.

"Some last minute things," she says.

"He depends on you."

"He says he does, yes."

"Then it's good you are there to help him."

Feng-qi has arranged for Claudia to watch the boys after school, because he had anticipated that Jessica would be back at work. And because Claudia needed the money—having lost her husband and her job at the same time, and very nearly losing her condo as a result. And because she got along well with the boys. It had seemed like an ideal situation, despite the expense. He's been thinking, though, that Jessica's recent moroseness might be due in part to her own unemployment and having few responsibilities around the house. He has been doing most of the cooking, he was caring for his father, he even cleaned. He doesn't blame her for not wanting to continue at the bookstore, although she had in the past claimed to enjoy it there. He has assured her that he fully understands, but the truth is that he does not. He has even tried to talk to her about this, but she deflects him. Now, though Claudia will be unhappy, he is thinking that Jessica should at least watch the children after school. Her work with the novelist is flexible. She has the time.

Jessica phones him at work. Simon's teacher has called the apartment and wants to meet with them as soon as possible. The next afternoon they go together to pick Simon up from school and they sit in his classroom, in the tiny schoolhouse chairs, with Mrs. Praisner standing above them like a looming, tweedy giant. Simon waits with a teacher's aide on the playground.

"I'm afraid he's been fighting," says Mrs. Praisner.

"That's not like Simon," Feng-qi says.

"Lately, I'm afraid it is. He hit another boy because of something he said."

"Said what?"

"That Simon's mother is dead."

"As you know, she died in an accident, a little over a year ago."

"What he said exactly was, 'your mother's dead and she's not coming back.' And that's when Simon punched him."

The incident at the school gives Feng-qi the idea that the time has come to move. Originally, Maddie had chosen this building in this neighborhood because she wanted to expose the boys to diversity and to the arts, and Feng-qi had agreed, with some reluctance, that they would benefit. But he's no longer certain they were right. Although the neighborhood has seen improvement, it still seems dangerous, and, after Simon had admitted to Feng-qi that a teenager had stolen his watch in the alley, the boys were no longer allowed to wander outside by themselves. It's no place for children, or at least not his children, and he worries about Jessica's safety, too. Isn't an attractive young woman vulnerable?

Without telling Jessica—he understands that this is a risk, that she would prefer to be consulted on a matter this important, but he believes she will enjoy the surprise—Feng-qi begins looking at houses in the far suburb of Annandale with the help of a local Chinese-American realtor, second generation, like Jessica. There is a large population of Asians in the area, an abundance of Asian groceries and restaurants, plus public schools where Simon and Wesley won't feel out of place and Jessica can make friends. She'll come to love the area, and so will they.

He sees three that he thinks will work. Before he can discuss the move with Jessica, however, one of the houses is taken off the market and the second is sold. The realtor is blunt: he must act fast.

Feng-qi is in Philadelphia for a conference at which he is presenting the data from a new report to be issued by his bureau in the Labor Department. It is the first time he has left the boys with Jessica overnight, and he didn't want to do it, but the conference is important. And she's their mother now; they must all grow to love each other, sooner rather than later. He tries not to worry.

He is waiting his turn to deliver his presentation when his cell phone rings. He's aware of the stares he draws as he tries to silence the phone and escape the auditorium. In the anteroom, he answers the call from Claudia. He listens, hears static on the line and something in Claudia's voice—it's pitched high, and, while she's normally calm and methodical, now she's speaking so fast it's hard for him to understand—alarms him. She's in the Emergency Room at G.W. Hospital with Wesley who's running a high fever. She doesn't know where Jessica is. She had knocked on the novelist's door because she often goes there to work on the man's book, but there was no answer. Claudia hadn't known what else to do.

Feng-qi leaves the conference. There isn't time to tell anyone; he just gathers his belongings, checks out of the hotel, and goes.

While he's en route, Claudia calls with updates. Doctors suspect a virus. Still no word from Jessica. They're giving him antibiotics. Susanna from next door has agreed to watch Simon when he gets home from school. Wesley is resting, and they're going home. Feng-qi changes course and heads for Nanking Mansion.

The apartment is quiet when Feng-qi enters. His arms ache from his tight grip on the steering wheel and his leg is stiff from the steady pressure on the gas pedal as he sped down I-95. Jessica is sitting in the kitchen, sipping tea, lit only by the lamp over the stove.

"Wesley's okay," he says. He doesn't go to her. The overnight bag still in his hand anchors him.

"Yes. He's fine. Sleeping."

"I was worried."

"He's fine now."

"Claudia couldn't find you."

"I was working."

"I was worried."

"I'm sorry," Jessica says. "But everything's fine."

"No," Feng-qi says. "I don't think it is." He hears that his voice is too loud, that anger, an emotion he seldom expresses, is burning in him, like Wesley's fever. He turns away.

They go out to eat at their favorite restaurant, Mario's, leaving the boys with Claudia. Since the scare of Wesley's fever, which passed as quickly as it arose, they've spoken little, and Feng-qi thinks they need to take this break. He wishes they could go away somewhere, just the two of them, on a kind of honeymoon, like the trip he and Maddie took to Chicago, but that's out of the question because of work and the boys. So a night out will have to do, for now. Jessica is staring at the menu and doesn't answer when the waiter asks for their orders, but when Feng-qi chooses the shrimp scampi she tells the waiter she'll have the same. Feng-qi looks at her. She never eats shrimp. She never orders the same thing he does.

He says, "There's something I wanted to talk about," at the same time that she says "We need to talk." He smiles at the coincidence, but she doesn't.

"You first," she says. She sips her water.

"All right. I thought we could save a little money if you watched the boys after school, instead of paying Claudia to do it." He feels badly for Claudia, who needs the money they pay her, but he'll help her find something else that will make better use of her experience in advertising.

Jessica nods, still holding the water glass to her lips, but Feng-qi has the impression that she isn't listening.

"There's something else," he says.

And then he tells her he's made an offer on a house.

"*Hao ma*?" Is that okay? Since his father's death, Jessica has stopped studying Chinese. He wants her to keep using it, for the boys' sakes, and so for simple expressions he sometimes slips into Mandarin. "*Hao bu hao*?" Okay or not?

She nods again. They sit silently while the food is set in front of them. Jessica stares at her shrimp.

"The thing is, now that the book is done," she says, "Nathan is moving back to Paris."

For a moment, Feng-qi is pleased with the implication of Nathan's impending move and he smiles—one less thing to worry about, nothing to interfere with their move to the suburbs, and with that distraction out of the way Jessica will have plenty of time for the boys—until he realizes, as if he is hearing the delayed report of a distant gun, what is coming next.

"He's asked me to go with him."

Has he heard right? The restaurant is loud. Did he misunderstand?

"Why would he ask this of you? The work is done, you said. For the next book he can find another . . . helper."

"It's more than that, Feng."

Wind. He knows she's trying to be gentle. She calls him that in quiet times, when she clings to him. And now what he had not wanted to see becomes clear.

"I'm not blind," he says, although that's exactly what he's been. "I've seen you with him. It isn't so hard to figure out what he is to you. But I don't understand why. Why would you do this to us?"

"I'm sorry," she says. "But I have to."

"Just come with me to see the house."

"I'm sorry."

He stands in an autumn shadow, the new house looming behind him. The brick wall that surrounds the garden reminds him of the walled courtyard of the old houses in China, the kind that are now mostly gone. In the corner, in a tangle of ivy, is a mossy bench. He brushes away leaves and acorns, and sits. It is the kind of garden his father would have loved, where he could grow vegetables as in those long ago days. He might have built a small pond, a waterfall. Feng-qi pictures a bird-feeder in the shape of a pagoda. His father could sit on the bench and watch colorful carp in the pond, visited by finches and sparrows, and allow himself to be transported to a time before everything changed, before the sea rose and covered the earth, before the wars, before flying here into the nothingness that his life became.

There is room enough in this house for the boys, for Claudia if she will come to help, for Maddie's mother when she chooses to visit. And there is more than enough room for the ghost of Maddie herself, and his father, and all of his ancestors, wherever they are.

Clifford Garstang is the author of the prize-winning short story collection *In an Uncharted Country* (Press 53, 2009). His work has appeared in numerous literary magazines including *Bellevue Literary Review, Blackbird, Cream City Review, Shenandoah, Tampa Review,* and *Virginia Quarterly Review*, and has received Distinguished Mention in the Best American Series. He has received fellowships from the Virginia Center for the Creative Arts, Kimmel Harding Nelson Center for the Arts, and the Sewanee Writers' Conference. He holds an MFA in Fiction from Queens University of Charlotte and is the founder and editor of *Prime Number Magazine*. He is also the author of the popular literary blog *Perpetual Folly*.

After receiving a BA in Philosophy from Northwestern University, Garstang served as a Peace Corps Volunteer in South Korea, where he taught English at Jonbuk University. He then earned an MA in English and a JD, *magna cum laude*, both from Indiana University, and practiced international law in Chicago, Los Angeles, and Singapore with one of the largest law firms in the United States. Subsequently, he earned a Master of Public Administration from Harvard University's John F. Kennedy School of Government and worked for Harvard Law School as a legal reform consultant in Almaty, Kazakhstan. From 1996 to 2001, he was Senior Counsel for East Asia at the World Bank in Washington, D.C., where his work focused on China, Vietnam, Korea, and Indonesia.

Garstang teaches creative writing at Writers.com and elsewhere. He currently lives in the Shenandoah Valley of Virginia.

Cover artist **BenWill** (Benjamin Williamson) is a modern abstract expressionist painter living in Portland, Oregon. In reflecting on the philosophy behind his work, he explains, "I don't want my art to be about standing still, resting on any successes, and becoming complacent. So, it's important for me to always focus on expanding my work and extending myself on the canvas." BenWill's paintings are currently found in collections throughout North America, Europe, and Asia. Information about BenWill and his work can be found at www.benwill.com.

AUTHOR'S NOTE

Many people have helped make *What the Zhang Boys Know* possible, and I give them my deepest thanks:

Thank you to the Virginia Center for the Creative Arts, where much of this book was written, for providing the time, space, and environment to create. Thanks also to the support of the Sewanee Writers' Conference and the incredible faculty and staff who gather there every summer in Tennessee—my visits to the mountain have always given me inspiration.

Special thanks to Tim O'Brien, an amazing writer and mentor, who believed in this project and helped shape these stories. I will always be grateful.

I also owe a debt of gratitude to the members of the Zoetrope Virtual Studio where many of the stories in this book were reader-tested, and to the editors of the fine journals that published them. For most writers in the early stages of their careers, journals provide their sole publishing outlet, and the literary world would be much poorer without them. Please support literary magazines by subscribing.

My friend Mary Akers, a wonderful writer, provided immeasurable help by commenting on all of these stories at various stages of their development. Thank you, Mary.

Finally, I'd like to thank Kevin Watson, Editor and Publisher at Press 53, lover of short stories and all around great guy, for falling in love with *Zhang Boys*.

CPSIA information can be obtained at www.ICGtesting.com
Printed in the USA
LVOW05s1938240714

395877LV00009B/1157/P